"You always talk about family togetherness, but nobody's on my side," Dinah cried out. "All you think about is that I'm fat. Nothing else matters. I could find the cure for cancer and it wouldn't matter, because I'm fat. . . ."

Dinah really started to cry. When she saw her parents moving towards her, she couldn't stand it. She had to get away, and she knew where she would go—to the edge of the woods where her special tree was, to the warm, safe world of the Green Fat Kingdom. . . .

ISABELLE HOLLAND grew up in Switzerland, Guatemala, and England. She came to the United States at the age of twenty to finish college at Tulane University in New Orleans. Since then she has worked in New York City, mainly in publishing. She is the author of several books including *Alan and the Animal Kingdom; Heads You Win, Tails I Lose; Hitchhike; The Man Without a Face;* and *Of Love and Death and Other Journeys;* all available in Dell Laurel-Leaf editions.

LAUREL-LEAF BOOKS bring together under a single imprint outstanding works of fiction and nonfiction particularly suitable for young adult readers, both in and out of the classroom. Charles F. Reasoner, Professor of Elementary Education, New York University, is the consultant to the series.

Dinah
and the
Green Fat Kingdom

Isabelle Holland

Published by
Dell Publishing Co., Inc.
1 Dag Hammarskjold Plaza
New York, New York 10017

Laurel-Leaf Library ® TM 766734,
Dell Publishing Co., Inc.

ISBN: 0-440-91918-5

RL: 5.0

Reprinted by arrangement with J. B. Lippincott Company
(a division of Harper & Row, Publishers, Inc.)

Printed in the United States of America

First Laurel-Leaf printing—March 1981

ONE

The hassle about my weight, which had been building ever since we moved to this town last year, came to a new head the afternoon Mother came into the kitchen and found me scraping up the last of the chocolate batter Mrs. Lewis had left for me. Luckily, I thought, snatching my finger out of the bowl, I had managed to eat almost all of it before Mother charged through the door.

"Why on earth are you eating that junk?" Mother said. She put her packages on the kitchen table. "Dinah, how could you? You know what Dr. Brand said."

I did. After weeks of talking about my weight, Mother had dragged me to see him the previous week. Dr. Brand, who is a pediatrician, had said that a twelve-year-old girl, four feet, ten inches, should weigh no more than ninety pounds tops—which meant, since I had just tipped the scale at one hundred and twenty-two, that I had to lose at least thirty-two pounds.

"So I'm chubby," I'd muttered, getting off the scale in his examining room. "Big deal."

He'd handed me a printed diet. "It's long past chubby, I'm afraid," he'd said. "I'll explain the diet to you back in my office. The most important thing to remember is, no snacks. Of any kind. Whatever." To make sure I didn't forget, he'd repeated it to Mother, who'd been waiting for us in his office.

Now, starting to put away some of the groceries, Mother reminded me. "He said no snacks ever, Dinah, remember? And here I find you eating cake batter, which is about ninety percent sugar." She glanced reproachfully at Mrs. Lewis. "And you know you shouldn't encourage Dinah to eat that sugary stuff at all, let alone between meals. You *know* she's trying to lose weight."

"No—" Mrs. Lewis eased her cakes out of the baking pans— "I don't know that she's trying to lose weight. I know that you're trying to get her to lose, but that's different."

Mother closed her lips in a certain way usually described in books as "firm." "Well, I don't want you giving her any more cake mix or cookies or homemade candy, or, for that matter, anything at all between meals."

"It's pretty hard to tell her she can't have something when Brenda and Tony and Jack are in here eating the leftovers of the cake batter."

"They don't have a weight problem. Suppose she were a diabetic? Would you feed her sweets then?"

"That's different," Mrs. Lewis said.

"No, it's not. That's where you're wrong. And in future," Mother went on, "I would like you to do as I ask as far as Dinah's eating between meals is concerned."

"Then you'll have to tell the others that they'll be refused, too," Mrs. Lewis said, smoothing icing with her spatula. "Maybe it's possible for you to let them have cookies while you're refusing Dinah, but it's not possible for me. So either they all have it, or none."

As I heard Mother slam the cabinet door, I looked with warm approval at Mrs. Lewis. She had small green eyes in a large red face, and a big pink body packed tightly into a white uniform. She knew I shouldn't be eating the cake batter, and she knew that I knew I shouldn't, and I knew that she knew that I knew. The one thing I didn't know was why she refused flatly to tell me not to. Everybody else was always telling me not to eat whatever I happened to have in my mouth at the moment—unless, of course, it was something naturally repulsive like brussels sprouts or string beans—but I wasn't going to question my good luck. She and Brewster, Tony's black Labrador, were the only two creatures in the house who didn't take a personal and untiring interest in my weight problem. There are times, lately, when I think that if the Randall family didn't have my weight to have emotional crises over, life would be dull.

One of the problems is that since medical tests have proved that my being overweight does not spring from a physical cause—and therefore must be because of something psychological—Mother feels it's some kind of reproach that one of her four is (in her own words to Daddy, which I once overheard) "a walking statement of somebody's failure—probably mine."

Mother is medium height, slender and has a flat chest, which makes her look even more slender. My cousin Brenda, who is ten, two years younger than I am, looks exactly like her. Both have curly brown hair and brown eyes. My brothers Donald, Tony and Jack are also thin. Tony, who is sixteen, and Donald, who is eighteen and away at college, look like Daddy, with blond hair and gray eyes. Jack is nine. He has brown hair and gray eyes. They are all, including both parents, very good-looking, which is a sore trial for me, because I'm not. I have straight red hair and green eyes, and I'm short and fat. No matter what I do—except, of course, starve myself—I put on weight.

Now Mother glared at Mrs. Lewis and Mrs. Lewis pretended to ignore her. All three of us, there in the kitchen, knew that Mother would dearly love to fire Mrs. Lewis. Mother once said that her dream is to hire a first-rate nutritionist who would take an interest in my weight problem. Unfortunately, as my father pointed out, first-rate nutritionists do not come with a salary that we are able to pay. Furthermore, Mrs. Lewis is the only help Mother has found, so far, who always arrives by eleven o'clock in the morning, so that no matter how early any of us comes home from school, we aren't coming into an empty house. This, Mother says, is more important than anything else, because she doesn't get home from her job until nearly six. (Mother is something called an Economic Analyst with the biggest local bank.) So, though Mrs. Lewis may be horribly uncooperative about my weight problem, she's *there* and she's reliable. And when— Mother says—you have two working parents, reliability is above the price of rubies.

I could almost feel Mother reminding herself of this as she slapped the groceries into the cabinets and refrigerator. When she saw me standing there absently eyeing the now empty mixing bowl, she said, "And you might give me some help in putting these away."

I started handing her things. "Are you sure," I asked, pursuing an old line of thought, "that I wasn't adopted?"

"Lambie," Mother said, which is something she calls me when she has forgotten about my number-one problem, "if there's one thing a woman knows about without question, it's whether or not she's had a baby. Especially you."

"Why especially me?"

"Because, you know, you were a surprise package—I mean you weren't what you could call planned—and you raised every kind of ruckus in the months before your birth. Why," Mother went on, folding the brown paper bags and putting them in the broom closet, "I'll never really know. Having Donald and Tony was a breeze. I'd have said it was because you came so much later and I was older, except that Jack, who came after you, was also a breeze. Anyway, honey, you're *not*, positively *not*, adopted. Why do you keep thinking you are?"

"Because all the others look like you and Daddy. And like each other. I don't."

"You sound as though you want to be an orphan, an adopted waif."

"I do. There's no use in looking hurt, Mom. I've always said I do. At least it would explain things."

"Such as?"

"Such as having red hair when nobody in the family has, and—"

"I've told you before, your grandmother, my mother, had red hair. I realize that ever since you've known her it's been white. But it *was* red."

"And I'm the only one who has a weight problem," I went on.

"I think a couple of hot fudge sundaes a day, not to mention the odd candy bar here and there, and a package or so of chocolate-chip cookies, plus large helpings of peanut butter, might be called an explanation."

"Other kids have them, too."

"You know," Mother said, "you make me feel like the nag of all time."

She paused, obviously hoping I'd contradict her. But I couldn't. It's not that I don't love her, or love Daddy. It's just that they—especially Mother—don't seem to be able to think about anything but my weight. So, when I'm around them, I can't either.

All of a sudden I was sick of it all. And for the umpteenth time I considered running away.

"Where are you going?" Mother asked, as I ambled towards the door.

"To my room."

"Dinah—" Mother looked at me. "I really do hate being a nag. But I know that if you don't conquer this problem now, you'll have it—"

I didn't hear the rest, largely because I was halfway up the stairs. And I'd heard it all before.

When I got upstairs to my room I found Brenda there, doing her homework. It's not enough, I thought bitterly, that I have to have a cousin who weighs about seventy-five pounds and is the leading star of our local ballet school. She also gets straight A's.

Brenda is half an orphan. Her mother and father were divorced, and right after that her mother, who was my mother's sister, was killed in an accident. Since Brenda's father, my Uncle George Morris, is a mining engineer and is always being sent places like Afghanistan and Patagonia, Brenda lives with us. Which means she lives in my room, or what would have been my room. There weren't any extra bedrooms available. If she'd been a boy she would have gone in with Jack. But she was a girl, so I had the pleasure, and now it's *our* room.

"Hi," she said when I walked in. She was sitting at her neat desk in her neat half of our bedroom.

"Hi." One of the things I'm going to have when I run away is a room to myself, and it can be all sloppy, instead of just half sloppy the way it is now.

"I've just written a piece about Abraham Lincoln," my genius roommate said. "Can I read it to you?"

It was funny, I thought, how I'd never really liked Lincoln. "I have to go out," I said.

"I got an A on the report I did last week on the causes of the Civil War."

"Great!" I could feel a low, hollow sensation inside. I knew I was full of chocolate batter. Yet I felt hungry. My eyes slid to my closet, where my laundry bag was hanging. At the bottom of the laundry I'd hidden some candy bars and cookies.

"I've copied it out three times," Brenda said, holding up the two pages so I could see them. "Mrs. Simmons always says that how something looks is very important. Do you think she'll like it?"

Since everybody in the house knows that I am constantly having to do things over because of sloppiness, it was obvious that Brenda was deliberately pushing my inferiority button. I peered at the sheets, hoping that I could find something, anything—a small blot or a scratched-out word, a misspelling—that I could point to. Naturally, there was nothing.

"Congratulations," I said. "You're perfect." And I left the room before I did something like kick her. With a little luck, I thought, I could get outside without anyone's seeing me. But as I was running downstairs, luck failed me.

"Hello, Daddy," I said, as I saw him come in.

"Hi." He took off his raincoat and hung it in the hall closet. "Mother home?"

"Yes. She's in the kitchen, putting away groceries."

"I hope any help you gave her was not too enthusiastic," Daddy said jovially.

"Meaning you hope I didn't eat anything."

As he passed, Daddy gave me a whack on the fanny. "Let's not be so sensitive," he said. "The others home?"

"Brenda is upstairs. She's written a piece on Abraham Lincoln. I bet she'd read it to you if you asked."

"Did she read it to you?"

"No. She offered to, but I had something else to do."

"Such as?"

"I have an errand," I said hastily. " 'Bye."

"Dinner's in an hour," he called after me. "Don't be late."

"Maybe I ought to skip it," I said, thinking that at last he and I would agree. And if I missed dinner I would, somehow, sneak off to the village for a pizza.

"Three meals a day and no snacks. Isn't that what Dr. Brand said?"

Even though I was halfway down the road I heard that, though I pretended not to.

Our house is at the edge of town. Back of it are fields, and back of them are rolling hills and woods. I was never supposed to go there by myself, but I always did. To keep anyone from catching on, I started out pretending to go in the opposite direction, towards town and the common and the school and the library. But just as I reached the bend in the road leading in that direction, I ducked down a little alley that leads between two houses and cuts back through the fields. Then I ran through the first field, up the hill and into the woods. My tree was in the middle, near a huge stump, and sitting on a little mound by itself.

I knew that soon the sun would go down, and that, the moment that happened, I'd better be on my way back, because the family would be having fits about where I might be. But first I needed some time in my Green Kingdom.

My tree, which is a big oak, has a funny shape. Its trunk goes straight up for about seven feet. Then it has one main fork, with half the tree going in one direction and the other half going in the other. But the leaves are so thick that you can't see up beyond that. Anyway, it's the second fork, invisible from the ground, that is my personal area—I call it the Green Kingdom. And it's the most private place in the world.

Glancing around to make sure that no one was near—which was silly, because nobody ever was, but I had to be sure—I went around to the other side of the tree, where the roots were thicker. There, there were stones scattered around on the ground. I bent down and lifted one that was sitting between two raised pieces of root. Underneath that stone was a smaller one. I lifted that, too. And underneath the second was a hole. I put my hands in the hole and pulled up one of those foot rules that carpenters use, the kind that straightens into one long piece. At one end I had glued and taped a hook. Unfolding the ruler to its yard length, I went back around the tree, held the ruler up as high as I could and fished around among the branches until I felt what I was looking for. Then I pulled, and down came a rope. I folded the ruler and put it back into the hole and took out a small canvas airline bag with a long strap, which I put over my shoulder.

With my feet braced against the trunk of the tree, I hauled myself up until I had reached the first fork. At that point I stopped and pulled the rope up so it couldn't be seen from below. Then, taking the right side of the fork, I climbed easily up to the second fork, which was big and flat, and sat down. Then I sighed and patted the branch above my head.

"Thank you, tree spirit," I said.

It was my brother Jack who discovered the big oak. That was about a year ago, a few weeks after we'd moved into the house. He came home with a broken arm after trying to climb it.

"You were an idiot to try to climb that tree," my father said in disgust when the whole family took Jack to the hospital. "Find one nearer your size and talents."

Jack is stubborn, like me. But after trying the tree once more, and falling once more and having to have his arm reset, he decided to put the tree house Daddy had made for him in the elm at the back of the garden.

"Would you make *me* a tree house?" I asked Daddy the night after he'd finished Jack's tree house. I was in the kitchen helping Mother get dinner ready. But Mother had gone into the dining room and Daddy and I were alone. He was busy stowing his tools in the cabinet just outside the kitchen.

"What would you want with a tree house, honey?"

"The same as Jack wants with his," I said. "To sit in it."

"Well," Daddy said, and he glanced quickly at me. "Maybe when you're a little thinner. Getting up trees requires agility."

Unfortunately, Tony came into the kitchen just as Daddy finished talking and wanted to know what was going on. Daddy, with a smile, told him. And I stood there between them wishing I'd never asked.

But, later, when I went up to look at the huge oak tree, I thought maybe they were right. That seven or eight feet of trunk didn't have one decent foothold. And the branches of the fork slanted up so steeply that I couldn't see a way to get a rope over one of them. I decided at that moment that the tree was probably a sacred tree like the ones the Druids had. (I had read about the Druids in a book on mythology lent me by Miss Bolton, who used to be my Sunday School teacher.) And if that were the case, it would explain why nobody could climb it: the tree would have a spirit that would repel any invader.

I put both hands out and laid them against the bark and wondered if somewhere the tree had a heart that beat and whether, if I stood there long enough and quietly enough, I would feel it. Then I heard my voice say, "If you really don't want to be climbed, I won't bother you." And that I sat down beneath the tree, with my fanny in a round seat made by the roots. Right in front of me was the old stump, but on either side I could see the fields leading down to our street, and the roofs of the houses, which were pink and dark red and brown, and then, far in the distance, on the other side of the river, the city where my father works. The stump really blocked the view. But in a funny way it made me feel more private.

Behind me, on the opposite side of the tree, the ground dipped a little and then rose steeply, and on top of that hill was the Van Hocht house, called by everybody the neighborhood eyesore.

As I sat and looked out over the town, I thought about the spirit of the tree and decided that if I died I'd like to become a tree spirit. If I were a tree spirit I wouldn't have a body, and bodies, as far as I was concerned, were bad news.

I don't know what happened to me then. I must have dozed off, because I had a dream. I dreamed that the tree spirit, who had a voice rather like Miss Bolton's, only younger, spoke to me and said, "Dinah, I don't like people climbing up me. But because you're different, I'll make an exception. Somebody once put a rope around one of my branches, only it's wrapped around and hidden where you can't see it. I want you to walk around me three times, then put your arms around me and shake me."

I knew when I woke up that I had dreamed, and thought how odd it was that the tree spirit would have the same voice as Miss Bolton. Slowly I got to my feet, but I didn't move. I just stood there, looking up at the tree. *I want you to walk around me three times, then put your arms around me and shake me.* The words were as clear in my head as they had been in my dream. How silly, I thought. Anybody watching would think I was crazy. But I walked around the tree three times. When I got back to where I'd started from, I looked up into the leaves, and then, stepping as close as the roots would let me, I put my arms around the trunk and rested my cheek against the rough bark. Then I kissed the tree, and shook it as much as I could.

I didn't expect anything to happen, so I tried not to feel let down when it didn't. "Anyway, thank you for the dream," I said. And I walked back to the house.

It was the next day that the spooky thing happened. When I got up to the tree I saw something lying against the trunk. At first I thought it must be a long snake of some kind, and what fun it would be to put it in Brenda's bed. But I forgot about that when I realized it was a dirty, frazzled-looking rope. Some ratty kids had been up disturbing my tree, I thought, taking the rope in my hands and looking at it.

At that moment I remembered the dream and I stood there, staring down at the rope. "I don't believe it," I said slowly.

The leaves of the tree rustled as the wind moved through them. "I'm sorry," I said, as I thought about the spirit of the tree and how I might have hurt her feelings. "But you have to admit that it's highly improbable." Which is one of my father's favorite expressions when anybody asks him about things like UFOs and souls and psychic manifestations.

Experimentally I pulled on the rope. Then I pulled harder, and harder still. In spite of its crummy appearance, it seemed solid. So slowly, and puffing and panting and pressing my sneakers against the bark of the tree, and getting my jeans rubbed and stained and snagged, I hauled myself up to the first fork. Then I stood up in it.

It was like looking into another world—a great beautiful green and gold world, strung together with brown limbs. I had known the tree was huge, but not *this* huge. And it was incredible the way it hid this inside world from down below. I could see, but no one could see me. Nobody knew I was there. . . .

I never told anyone that I had climbed the tree, not even Dottie, who is sort of my best friend. I say "sort of" because I really don't like her that much, but she's fat like me, which means we're always stuck together at school. She lives two blocks away and I see her more than anybody else.

After a while I got so I could climb up that rope without one puff or pant. I started keeping a notebook wrapped in plastic under the stone. I "borrowed" one of the canvas airline bags lying around the basement, and with it, I could haul things up into the tree without too much trouble. In the notebook I wrote ideas and descriptions and things that made me mad. And then I began putting in stories about the Green Kingdom and the Green People. Each day I'd write a different story.

Now, almost a year after I'd discovered the tree, there were three notebooks full and I was working on the fourth. There were lots of different stories, but the main thing about the Green People was that they were fat, and all the Beautiful Green People were particularly fat. The Green Princess, who was the most beautiful and sought-after girl in the Green Kingdom, was the fattest of all.

I'd discovered the tree at the beginning of the first summer we were in the house. By the time autumn came, I was so used to going to it almost every day that I could hardly bear to think about the coming winter, when the leaves would fall off. And I kept waiting and waiting for the first signs. Each day I'd turn up under my tree expecting to be able to see inside it—but as the other trees got barer and barer, my oak stayed exactly the same. I was afraid to ask at home if oaks were the kind of trees that lost their leaves, in case I might arouse suspicion. But I took one of the leaves to the botanical wing in the local museum, and I found that this particular kind of oak kept its leaves all winter.

"It's called a canyon or gold cup oak," the nice man in the museum said, turning the leaf over in his hands. "We're pretty far north for a live oak, but there are some in this area. Where is it?"

"Over on the other side of town." I was astonished to hear myself lie. But I was terrified that he would go and look at it.

So I had my tree world all winter, too. And now it was spring. And I sat in my tree thinking about the Beautiful Fat People and the Green Fat Kingdom, where I was never considered fat enough, and then I drifted off into my other fantasy, where I'd be so thin that everyone—Mother, Daddy, Tony, Dr. Brand and Miss Boyer, the athletics teacher at school—would be pleading with me to have a second helping.

"Please have a potato, Dinah. You must build yourself up. . . ."

"You'd be so pretty, Dinah, if only you were heavier. . . ."

"I want everyone to watch how lightly Dinah vaults over the horse. . . ."

That last voice definitely came from Miss Boyer, who was half English and had a sort of crisp accent. She was also tall and fair-haired, with the most beau-

tiful grown-up female body I'd ever seen. Sometimes
at night I would have a fantasy that someone would
appear and say to me, "If you nibble this just before
you go to sleep you'll wake up looking like Miss
Boyer." The someone who offered me the magic potion would sometimes be a witch or wizard, who often
looked like an ugly Miss Bolton, and sometimes he or
she (I was never quite sure which) would be from
another planet or galaxy. Anyway, in my fantasy I'd
take the magic potion and the next morning when I
came down to breakfast Daddy and Tony would just
stare at me, and Tony would say, "Dinah, I didn't realize how neat and cool you were getting to be. I'm
not ashamed anymore to have people at school know
you're my sister." And Daddy would put his arm
around me and say, "From now on anybody who's not
nice to Dinah will have to deal with *me*." Mother
would simply say, "Please, Dinah, darling, have another English muffin. I get so worried about your not
eating enough. . . ."

The Swiss cowbell that Mother had installed outside the kitchen door started clanking. I could hear it
right across the fields, and I knew that dinner would
be on in about twenty minutes.

Sighing, I climbed down the tree, put the rope back
up where I could hook it down easily again, and put
everything away. Then I went home.

"Where've you been?" Mother said.

"In the library," I replied, as I always did.

"I phoned the library and you weren't there,"
Mother said. I could tell by her voice that she was
angry. "I wanted you to pick up a quart of milk on

your way home. But the librarian there said you very rarely come in during the week. So I suppose all this time when you were telling me you were in the library, you were down in the village ice cream parlor with that fat little Dottie Marlow, both of you stuffing yourselves full of that sweet poison they hand out."

We were in the hall, about to go into the dining room. I didn't say anything, because I couldn't think what to say. Every afternoon when I said I'd been in the library I'd been in my tree, not the ice cream parlor. But if I told Mother that, she and the others would know about the tree, and it wouldn't be mine and private anymore. And they wouldn't rest until they found out how I got up into it. It was funny. Sometimes I could see a whole scene as though I weren't in it, and I was doing it now. There were Tony and his friends and some other kids from school standing around the tree watching me while I hauled myself up.

"Go to it, fatso!"

"Boy, she could use a derrick. . . ."

"Personally, I feel sorry for the tree. . . ."

I closed my eyes.

"You were in the ice cream shop, weren't you?" Mother said.

"Yes."

"Dinah, do you realize what you're doing to the rest of your life? Don't you want to be attractive? Don't you . . ."

Her voice faded as I tuned her out. I'd always been able to do that, but I was getting better and better at it.

". . . I've talked this over with your father and we've decided that we have to take drastic action. I'm sorry, Dinah, we don't want to act like jailers, but you're going to have to come straight home from school every day and then stay here. I've also spoken to Mrs. Lewis and she is strictly forbidden to let you have anything . . ."

I could feel the tears coming behind my eyes. I hated Mother and I hated Daddy, and I hated Tony.

"I'm sorry," Mother said. "I'm really sorry. But Dr. Brand said I was to keep after you until you took responsibility for yourself. I know you're humiliated—"

"Can I go now?" I said.

"We're going to have dinner."

"I'm not hungry." And, for once, I wasn't.

I didn't wait for her permission, I just went upstairs. But when I got to the top I remembered that Brenda the Successful would be up there, at least until she was summoned for dinner. I couldn't stand it. So I went instead to Jack's room. Jack is thin and a boy and my brother, all three bad. But he was better than Brenda.

"Can I come in?" I said outside his closed door.

The door opened. "Oh," he said. "It's you. Okay." And he walked away from the door, leaving it open. I went in and sat on his bed. Brewster, who actually belongs to Tony, but who likes Jack better and stays in his room, came over and shoved his nose against my hand.

"At least Brewster isn't always telling me to lose weight," I said.

Jack didn't say anything.

"You don't know how lucky you are," I said, sniffing.

"They're going to ground you for a while," Jack said. "I heard them talking."

"What I'd like to do is run away."

"Why don't you?"

"That's a big help," I said. "Where'd I go?"

"If it was me I'd go up to the Van Hocht place. There're lots of funny people up there. At least three of them are much fatter than you are."

I picked up Jack's teddy bear from his bed. "Fat is beautiful," I said.

"That's what she said."

"What?"

"Miss Van Hocht."

"When? I didn't know you knew her."

"I don't. I heard her say it when some kids laughed at her when she got off the bus at the bottom of the hill."

I shrank a little. "She must have hated them."

"Yeah. I'd have thought so. But she didn't sound like it. She sounded like she didn't care."

"Is she bigger than me?"

"Lots. You're not that big. You just look big compared to Brenda."

"Do you like Brenda?"

"No. She told Mom that Brewster chewed my sneakers. And if the phone hadn't rung, Mom would have said that Brewster couldn't stay in my room."

"Why is she such a *toad?*"

"Because she is."

"It's not fair. I'm not a toad, but I get picked on for being fat. She's not fat, but she's a toad. But nobody picks on her for that. Do you think anybody knows how toad-like she is except us?"

"Toads are nice," Jack said. "But I don't think any-body really sees how she is except us."

"Did you hear any more about what they're going to do to me?"

"They're going to send you to some nutrition place a couple of times a week and you're going to have to do exercises and learn about food."

I lay down on Jack's bed. Brewster got up and lay down beside me, snuffling. "Maybe I could get really sick and lose my appetite and die," I said. "Do you know of any diseases where people lose their appe-tites?" Jack is a bug about science.

"Lots. But you'd feel sick, so that wouldn't be any good."

"Dinner," Mom yelled from below. "Jack, Brenda, Dinah, come on down."

It would have been lovely to stay upstairs and make them all sorry. The trouble was, I was hungry.

TWO

Dottie and I were sitting in The Spot, an ice cream and candy parlor in the basement of one of the local department stores. The Spot, which is supposed to attract young people, is dreary and second-rate, and none of the kids at school would be caught dead in it. Which is why we went there. Everybody else sitting around the counter and at the tables was about fifty.

"So when do you go to this nutrition place?" Dottie asked, sucking on her straw.

"Tomorrow," I said. "Did I tell you they grounded me?"

"You don't seem very grounded now. I thought you were supposed to go straight home from school."

"I am. But I got out this morning before Mother remembered to remind me about it and make me promise to come straight home from school. She overslept and was afraid of being late to the bank, so I just stayed out of the way and kept a low profile. Anyway, she never comes here, and none of her friends do." I spooned up the last of my chocolate ice cream hot fudge sundae.

"You want anything else?" the waitress said, taking her pencil out of her hairdo.

I hesitated. What I wanted was another sundae, this time with butter pecan sauce. "Just a minute," I said, and reached into my bag for my wallet. I didn't have enough for another, because one of the bad things about The Spot was that in addition to being second-rate it was expensive. "No. I don't have enough money. I guess that'll be all."

"I'll lend you some," Dottie said.

It was a sore temptation. Ever since the row yesterday I'd been hungrier than ever. And Dottie's parents were rich. But just as I was going to say, "Okay, thanks," I looked at her practically gouging out her plate to get the last of her whipped cream. She had about three chins. But then, I thought, catching sight of myself in the mirror across from the counter, who was I to look down on Dottie because she had three chins? "No thanks. I really don't like to borrow."

"You borrowed fifty cents two weeks ago," Dottie said.

I was about to deny it, when I remembered that I had. I could feel myself getting hot. "Here," I said, taking fifty cents out of my wallet and handing it to her. It would mean I wouldn't have enough money for the bus. But paying my debt would be worth it.

"You don't have to pay me now," Dottie said. "I only said it to show how I don't mind your borrowing."

I knew it wasn't true. She'd said it because she knew I'd forgotten and would feel awful when I was reminded. For a moment I considered telling her I hated her and didn't want her for a friend. But then who would I have?

"No, I really don't want another," I said. "I have to go."

"Aren't you going home on the bus?"

"Later. I have errands to do."

"I'll go with you on the errand," Dottie said, following me out to the elevator. "I don't have to go for my fitting for another hour."

I didn't say anything, because having to have specially made clothes was something I didn't like to talk about. Sometimes store clothes for the "chubbies" were okay if they were let out a little. Mrs. Lewis did that. But occasionally my clothes had to be made from scratch, so Mother took me to Madame Jones, who was French and had married a GI in World War II.

"Who does your clothes?" I asked Dottie, pushing the button for the elevator. "Madame Jones?"

"No," Dottie said. "Mother has Carlo run them up for me." Carlo was a designer who owned the most expensive boutique in town. "Did Madame Jones do your jeans?"

"Yes," I said very quickly, because other people were now around us and there was something very shaming about dressmaker jeans. In fact, Mother hadn't wanted to have them made for me. "For your size and shape, Dinah, dresses look a lot better," she'd said. But none of the other kids wore dresses, so I'd held out for jeans and wore them with a loose blouse—also made by Madame Jones.

"My errand's going to take a long time," I said. I still hadn't figured out how I was going to get home on the bus. But I preferred to gamble that the driver would let me go for free rather than have Dottie find out I didn't have enough money. "Anyway, I have to go to the ladies' room first. And I'd rather go alone. It's sort of private."

Dottie's hazel eyes widened. "Did you get your period?"

I gritted my teeth and waited for her to stop talking. It was a crowded elevator.

"I haven't started yet," Dottie went on, as though we were the only two people for miles around. "When did you—"

"A year ago," I said quietly, and tried to will Dottie to shut up. It seemed to me that "a year ago" was, for me, like the year one, the start of the calendar, the beginning of everything. A year ago we moved to this town, I began menstruating, Brenda came to live with us, I started putting on the twenty pounds I had gained since then—and not long after that my family began to bug me about my weight.

Abruptly the elevator doors opened at the third floor.

"Good-bye," I said, and wiggled out just as the doors closed. Then, afraid that Dottie would somehow follow me by getting the next elevator, I went to the door marked STAIRS and ran up two flights. I took a different elevator to the tenth floor, where I got out and decided to stay until I had given Dottie a chance to leave the store.

"Can I help you, young lady?" a man's voice said.

I looked up. He was tall and had a lot of teeth and wore glasses and a badge that said MR. BOGGS, FLOOR MANAGER, and something told me that he was about to say children weren't allowed on the tenth floor by themselves. So I said quickly, "I'm going to meet my mother up here. I've just been to the ladies' room."

And then prayed that the ladies' room was on another floor.

"Oh. I see. Well, in which department were you to meet her?"

I looked around wildly. There seemed to be a knot of people in the far corner of the other side of the store. "Over there. Where all those people are," I said. "Thanks." And I walked off quickly.

Whatever those people were doing, I could get myself in the middle of them and wait until Mr. Nosey Boggs drifted away. Then I could look around for a while until Dottie had had a chance to get on the bus, and after that I would go home and face the music, whatever it was.

When I got up to the corner, I saw that there were a lot more people than I had thought; most of them were in a section behind some partitions. I squeezed myself around the partition and then saw that a pretty girl, who looked like a movie or TV star, was holding up a kitten. "Now who would like to start the bidding on this adorable ginger kitten?" she said.

"What's happening?" I whispered in the general direction of the woman standing next to me.

"An auction of strays, with the money to go to the local humane society."

I like animals, and my brother Jack is crazy about them, so I decided to stay and watch. After a while people started leaving, taking the animals they'd bought in cardboard containers, and I got nearer to the front. A tall thin woman on the other side of me bought a white and black dog with long ears and hair. Another woman bought a tan dog with a sad expression. Several cats were bought. Then the movie-star-type girl held up a fat, funny-looking puppy with a squashed-in face.

"He may not be beautiful, but he has a lovely soul," she said.

Silence. There were no takers.

"Please," she said.

The people who were left shifted around.

"Have you got any others?" one of them asked.

The girl sighed and put the puppy down. "Here," she said, holding up a rust-colored puppy with floppy ears.

Somebody bought her—it was a female—right away. Three more, one dog and two cats, were sold.

"Come on, now," the lady auctioneer said. "There's got to be a home for this fellow. If not—well, you know the humane society can't keep him forever. He'll have to go to the pound."

"He looks like a frog," somebody said. "If he's that ugly now, what'll he look like later?"

"Even uglier," one woman said, laughing. She was leaving with the ginger kitten.

The others drifted away.

"Will he really have to go to the pound?" I asked.

The lady auctioneer looked up, and I saw that she wasn't as young as she had seemed at first.

"Yes. He will. And it's such a pity. With a little love he'll be fine. He seems to have an inferiority complex."

"What do you mean?"

"I mean that when I went over to the shelter, all the others came running over expecting to be patted. Even the kittens. This one just sat and looked at me from the other side of the cage, as though he were expecting the worst."

"Why don't *you* take him?"

"Because I have four cats and three dogs and I've promised my husband faithfully that I will not adopt another."

She had put him in a cardboard carrier, but left it open at the top. I went over and looked down at him, and he stared glumly back at me.

"I only have twenty-three cents," I said. "Is that enough?"

She had started to close the carrier, but she straightened and looked at me. "What would your mother and father say?"

"I'm an orphan."

"But you have to live with somebody."

I hadn't thought about that. She was beginning to look doubtful. "I live with my grandmother. She loves animals, and she said she would give me a puppy for my birthday. I'll take this one instead."

"Ready for us to pack up these things?" Two workmen had turned up, wearing coats that said they were from the humane society. One of them indicated some empty carriers and pens.

"Yes. You can take them."

"What about him?" one of the men said, indicating the rejected puppy.

"Oh, this young lady's just bought him," she said. She leaned down, closed the top of the carrier, then picked it up and handed it to me. "Enjoy," she said.

As I took it, she went on, "I'm letting you have him against all the rules, because for me to take him back now would mean almost certain death for him in a few days. Will you promise me that you won't mistreat him or starve him or abandon him if things get tough? Do you give me your word?"

"I promise," I said.

"And that if there's any kind of trouble or you find you can't take care of him, you'll bring him back to the humane society?"

"Yes. I will. Truly."

She stared hard at me. "I believe you. I think you're that kind of person."

A marvelous warm feeling went through me. I wanted to touch her, to put my arms around her. But I just stood there, and then, out of the corner of my eye, saw Mr. Nosey Boggs.

"I have to go," I said.

She looked up and saw the floor manager approaching. "Because of him?" she said.

"Yes. I told him—" Suddenly, as I was on the verge of explaining to her that I had told the floor manager I was waiting for my mother, I remembered that I had told *her* I was an orphan.

"Pay no attention to him," she said, gathering up her bag and coat. "I don't think he approves of animals anyway. You should have seen his face when all the carriers were brought up." Then she straightened and looked at me. "All of a sudden it just hit me that you said you only had twenty-three cents, which you just gave for the puppy. How are you going to get home? Are you with somebody?"

"No." I, too, was wondering how I was going to get home.

"Here." She opened her bag and took out a bill.

"I hate to borrow," I said.

"It's not a loan. It's a present."

"Well, I don't need that much. Just bus fare." I stopped, feeling that I wasn't being very polite. "I don't mean to be rude," I added.

"It's all right. How much is bus fare?"

"A quarter."

She put back the five-dollar bill she'd been holding and held out a dollar bill. "I would feel a lot better if you took that," she said. "Please. Really. Do me a favor."

I took the bill. "I'd like to pay you back. Could you please write down your name and address in this notebook here?" I got a pad out of my bag and handed it to her.

"You must come from a long unbroken line of Puritan-ethic believers," she said, taking the pad and writing.

I looked at what she'd written down: JANET MADISON, ROYAL COURT THEATRE. "You *are* an actress," I said.

"That's right. I'm here with the repertory company. There you are." She handed the pad back to me. Then she glanced at the carrier in my hand. "One of my dogs is a pug. He looks not unlike your friend there. I guess that's why I was so anxious for somebody to adopt him. Same fat wrinkles. Same pushed-in face. I love it."

"Fat is beautiful," I said experimentally.

She smiled. "Especially in puppies."

It wasn't exactly what I had hoped she would say. I waited for her to say something else. But she didn't. I looked up. Mr. Nosey Boggs, who had stopped to talk to somebody on the way, was almost on top of us.

"Good-bye," I said quickly. And I almost ran across the floor. I had a feeling that he was going to ask Janet Madison if my mother had appeared, so I was glad when an elevator door opened.

When I got outside, I went and stood on the platform that most of the buses going back to the village took off from and waited for the bus that stopped at the bottom of our road. While I was waiting, I put down the carrier and opened the top. The puppy stared back at me. "What's the matter, pup?" I said. "Don't you believe that anything good is ever going to happen?"

Its ears went up. Even more wrinkles appeared in its forehead.

"What a funny-looking dog," a woman beside me said.

I could feel myself bristle. "I think he's beautiful."

The woman gave a tight, polite smile. "I guess it takes all kinds—"

At that moment another woman said loudly, "You're absolutely right. He *is* beautiful. Don't let anyone tell you he isn't." I turned and looked at her. She was the fattest woman I'd ever seen, about twenty times bigger than me. "He's very handsome and has a good personality." She put her hand down into the carrier and rubbed the puppy between his ears. He gave a little whimper and then licked her hand. A pang of jealousy went through me. I stuck my hand down and he licked it twice, smelled it, and then licked it again.

"You see?" the fat woman said.

With a screech of compressed air the bus came up and its doors flew open. Hastily I closed the carrier and picked it up. "In you get," the fat woman said to me.

She and I sat with the carrier between us. "What's his name?" she asked me, when the bus had started.

"I haven't named him yet."

"You should give him a name soon. He won't be a real person to you until you do."

I was still thinking about a name when the puppy started crying in a series of mournful yelps. People around us stopped talking.

"He probably hates the carrier," the fat woman said. "Why don't you hold him on your lap?"

I put the carrier down, opened it and took the puppy out. He promptly stopped crying and licked my hand.

A man across the way said, "Why don't you call him Jumbo? He'll probably be huge."

I heard myself say passionately, "I don't think size has anything to do with what a person's name should be." I saw his mouth open. "Or a dog's."

The puppy looked at me and his almost nonexistent tail gave a slight wiggle. It was so slight that I almost didn't see it.

"He wagged his tail at you," the fat woman said.

"His name is Francis," I said.

"Francis!" the man said. "That's no name for a dog. Why are you calling him that?"

"Because that's his name." I looked back at the man, who was on the point of talking again. "He just told me."

The man made a noise like a snort. I glared back at him and then looked down. "Francis?" This time the wiggle was more than slight. I could feel his whole hind end moving. Then he made a sort of whiffling noise and tried to stand up.

"Do you have a leash for Francis?" the fat woman asked.

"A leash? I don't need one. I'll put him back in the carrier when I have to get off the bus."

"Yes, but you'll be taking him for walks, and if you

don't put him on a leash he could—in fact, almost certainly would—get run over."

"Oh. I didn't think of that. No, I don't have one."

"Well, I have one at home. You can stop by there, if you live near enough, and I'll let you have it."

"Where do you live?" I asked.

"At the top of Grumble Hill. Where do you live?"

"Halfway down." I was thinking. "But if you live at the top, you must live in the Van Hocht place."

"That's right."

I suddenly remembered that Jack had told me three fat people lived there. I had my mouth half open to tell her this when I realized that it was not the kind of thing I could say.

She smiled at me. "I'm Amelia Van Hocht Smith. Smith is my married name, but after my husband died and I came back here, it seemed easier just to go back to using my old name. I live up there with my two sisters and one or two other people. And, of course, the animals."

I wondered if the "one or two other people" she'd mentioned were also members of her family, and thought what a funny way it was of putting it. I tried to imagine Mother saying, "I live with my husband, James, and one or two other people." And she would never say, "And, of course, Brewster." Because Mother didn't much like animals. She put up with Brewster because Tony had won him as a prize in an essay contest.

"What animals?" I said.

"Oh, cats; dogs; Apollo, who's a donkey; some gerbils and Hamlet, the hamster."

I tried to imagine it. "Are they all yours?" I asked.

She didn't say anything for a minute; then: "We all belong to one another. This is our stop."

I'd passed here on the bus dozens of times and never realized it was the stop for the Van Hocht house. I peered out the window. "I don't see your house."

"You can't from here. It's hidden by the curve of the hill and the bushes."

In a minute the bus drew to a stop. I put Francis back in the carrier and closed it and Miss Van Hocht and I got out. As we started to walk, there came from inside the carrier a whimpering noise followed by small scratching sounds. Since I didn't have a leash yet I decided to ignore them. But the noises rapidly became louder.

"He wants to get out," Miss Van Hocht said. "He probably wants to go to the bathroom."

I put the carrier down, opened it hurriedly and lifted Francis out. Miss Van Hocht was right. Francis promptly peed. "I'm surprised he didn't go in the box," I said. "He's too little to be trained, isn't he?"

"Maybe somebody's been trying."

I thought about what Janet Madison had said. "And maybe not too kindly. You're a good boy," I said now to Francis, by way of general encouragement. Francis, his personal business finished, waddled over in my direction and sat on his behind and looked at me.

"He looks worried," I said.

"He probably is." Miss Van Hocht picked up the empty carrier. "He's worried that you're not going to love him. He wouldn't put it like that, or know that that was what he was worried about. But at the bottom of his dog soul that's what it is."

I was astonished at what I said next, because I

didn't remember thinking it a minute before. "Maybe he thinks he's too ugly to be loved."

"Then you'll have to convince him beyond any doubt that it's not true, won't you?"

There was something about her saying that that bothered me, but for a minute or two I couldn't quite get hold of what it was. "Yes, I guess so," I said now, absently, still trying to figure out what it was that was disturbing me. "Come on, Francis, come over here," I said, and patted my knee.

He didn't move for a minute. Then he stood up, all at once, on his short legs, lurched forward a few steps, looked at me, and then came forward again. When he reached me I bent down, put out my hand and patted him on the head. Then I rubbed him between and around the ears. His back wiggled. He rose up on his hind legs, snorting and puffing, and licked my face.

"We can start moving in the direction of the house," Miss Van Hocht said. "He'll follow us."

I moved forward a few steps. Francis gamboled after me, ran ahead a short way, looked back, came back, turned, ran ahead, inspected all the weeds at the side of the road, came back for reassurance, got told all over again that he was loved and ran ahead again.

"He's going to need a lot of convincing," Miss Van Hocht said.

I looked up at her. "Convincing? What about?"

"That's he's not too ugly to be loved."

Everything fell into place then, and a spurt of anger went through me as I thought I understood what she meant. I burst out, "You mean I should reassure Francis about not being too ugly to be loved, because I should know?"

"Is that what you thought I said, or meant?"

I wished now I hadn't said anything, but I stared hard at her and said, "Yes."

We had stopped and were staring at each other. Miss Van Hocht might be immensely fat and have on a baggy tweed suit and an old-fashioned felt hat with the brim turned down, but there was something about her—maybe it was the crisp way she talked, maybe it was the straight look in her clear blue eyes—that made me wish more than ever that I had kept my mouth shut.

"You thought I was commenting on the way you look, didn't you?"

It was really queer. Her voice before had been cool and severe, like a teacher's when she really knows how to keep a class in line. But now it was different. It was still strong and clear, but very warm, and for a minute I forgot that she was an adult and I was a child. And even though her voice was warm, I knew she wasn't sorry for me, which I always hate. Before I knew it the tears were pouring down my cheeks, only it didn't seem to matter.

"I wasn't," she said. "After all, I'm much, *much* fatter than you are. And I don't care. I don't care whether I'm fat or thin or whether you are, or whether Francis is. Either I like you or I don't. And I do like you, so that's that. But I also know how you feel, because a long time ago I felt that way, too. And I know what it's like."

Even though I was crying hard I was really quite happy. As I mopped my face with some tissues I'd pulled out of my pocket, I nodded and suddenly laughed.

"That's better," Miss Van Hocht said.

Out of the corner of my eye I saw that I was standing on the road above the wood containing my tree. I stared down, and in a second I picked out the huge spreading shape, green in the midst of green.

"What are you looking at?" Miss Van Hocht asked.

"My tree," I said. She was the first person I'd mentioned it to, but it seemed right.

"Tell me about it," she said.

So, as we walked up to the house, I did.

"Yes," she said. "I had a Fat Kingdom, too. With a Fat King and a Fat Queen."

"What happened to them?"

"I guess they faded when I grew up."

I was so busy listening, I wasn't looking where we were going. Now I saw we had come through a white gate and were in front of a tall frame house with gingerbread around the top of the big porch and turrets on two of the towers. Around the house was a sort of small field with tall grass. Big trees grew around the house, and a broken swing hung from a lower branch of one of the trees.

"Once this was a lawn," Miss Van Hocht said. "Back on the other side was a tennis court, and behind that a croquet lawn. Here, watch the step. It's broken."

We were standing in front of a front door that was partly clouded glass. Miss Van Hocht turned the knob and we walked in. Francis, who'd been doing his run ahead—run back bit all the way up the hill, pranced into the hall, then sat down on his rump.

"It's a little untidy," Miss Van Hocht said.

I tried to imagine what Mother, who believed in everything in its place and a place for everything, would think. The hall was huge, but it must have been bigger once, before all the bookcases and books had been put there. The bookcases went up to the ceiling against every possible wall surface, and piles of books as tall as I was were stacked in front of every bookcase.

"My father was very fond of books," Miss Van Hocht said. "And we all like to read."

"I've never seen so many, except in the public library," I said. "And they're, they're—well, all over the place."

"Desmond started to arrange them a few years ago, and he's working his way through the house. He hasn't arrived at the front hall yet."

I wondered who Desmond was.

"Here's Desmond now," Miss Van Hocht said.

A very thin old man with white hair and half glasses on his nose came through what I saw was an archway between two bookcases.

"Desmond," Miss Van Hocht said, "I'd like you to meet—" She turned to me. "You never told me your name."

"Dinah Randall," I said. "How do you do," I added, producing my best manners.

"And this is Desmond LeBreton," Miss Van Hocht said. "He came to help us with our books some years ago and moved in because it was so much more convenient."

"Did you bring any books?" Desmond asked.

"No. But I have lots at home."

He tilted his head back and peered at me through his half glasses. "You like reading?"

"Yes. Love it."

"Writing?"

I thought of the notebooks in the hole beside the tree root. I'd never told anyone about them. "Yes," I said, and I could feel myself blush. Somehow in this strange, comfortable house, I didn't mind talking about my notebooks.

"What kind of writing? I'd like to see—" Desmond started, when Francis, who had been sniffing around his foot, suddenly attacked his shoelace. He looked down, pushed up his spectacles and said accusingly, "Who's that?"

"That's Francis," I said. "I just bought him, and I came up here because Miss Van Hocht said she'd lend me a leash for him." I thought I'd better mention it, because I was fairly sure she'd forgotten.

But I was wrong. Miss Van Hocht, who'd opened a drawer in a chest squashed between two bookcases, said, "Here it is. I thought I'd put it there. If the cats are arriving perhaps you'd better pick up Francis. He might not have had the experience of having his nose scratched before, and his eyes are a bit prominent, aren't they? I suspect he has quite a bit of pug in him."

"Cats?" I asked, hastily picking up Francis and tucking him under my arm. Desmond, I noticed vaguely, had disappeared.

"Behind you."

I turned. Approaching down a narrow hall were more cats than I had ever seen at one time in my life. Some were kittens and were running and tumbling over one another. Others came at a stately pace. They were every color—black and white and gray and striped and calico—and long- and short-haired.

"How many do you have?" I asked.

"As of a week ago there were forty-two. But Cleopatra has had her litter since then, and Sebastian brought home The Black Panther, so we're not entirely sure. Ah—here come the dogs."

All of a sudden there was a tremendous commotion out in the back somewhere—several dogs barking at different pitches. I heard a door in the back open, and the barks hurtled closer. I clung more tightly to Francis. Something the size of a pony covered with black fuzzy hair and barking in a deep bass voice plunged out of the little hall. The air suddenly seemed full of cats as they leapt onto everything they could find. A couple of them clambered up into the space between the top of a row of books and the shelf above it.

"Silly," Miss Van Hocht said, coming over with a collar and leash and buckling the collar onto Francis's fat neck. "The cats act as though they think Diablo will kill them, whereas all any of them has to do is spit and he'll fly. He's all noise, aren't you, Diablo?"

"Whooff!" boomed Diablo, slavering as he lunged up to sniff Francis's rear end, while I held the puppy over my head.

"Will he hurt him?" I gasped.

"Not a bit. Put him down on the floor. You'll see!"

But I had become extremely attached to Francis in the hour or so since I'd bought him for twenty-three cents. "I'm afraid to."

Suddenly Miss Van Hocht was on top of me. The next thing I knew she'd taken Francis out of my hands and put him on the floor.

"You have to take risks, you know," she said.

Maybe so, I thought, but I stayed near in case I had to snatch Francis up again. Slowly, making low rumbling noises, the huge dog circled Francis, who turned just as slowly, keeping his protuberant eyes on the potential enemy. Then Francis barked. It was really just a little yap. But the big dog leapt back, hurtled down the narrow hall and disappeared.

"See?" Miss Van Hocht said.

After that I met Miss Agnes Van Hocht and Miss Alice, who were shorter than Miss Amelia but just as fat. They were sitting out in the large, sunlit kitchen preparing vegetables for dinner.

"Have a cookie," Miss Agnes said, offering me a plate of chocolate-chip cookies. I had thought I was quite hungry, but I didn't seem to be so now, and refused.

"In that case, I'll have one." Miss Agnes reached out a pudgy hand and took it. "Pull up a chair and I'll give you some potatoes to peel."

I'd never peeled potatoes before, though I liked them, especially with butter. Sitting down, I picked up a small potato and started peeling it. Whenever we had potatoes at home, I thought, there was nearly always a row when I took seconds. My father would say, "You've had enough of those, Dinah." And I'd say, "Well, Tony's had seconds." And Mother would say, "That's different." And I'd say, "It's not fair." And Tony would say, "Don't you want boys to find you attractive? No boy I know will ever look at you if you stay that fat." And I'd say, "All you ever think about is sex." And Tony would say, "Maybe it's time you thought more about it." And Daddy would bellow, "That's enough!" And I burst into tears and go upstairs.

Maybe that, or something like that, had only happened once or twice, but it seemed like a lot of times. I looked at Miss Agnes, the shortest and fattest of all, placidly running her knife around a potato.

"Do you like potatoes?" I asked her.

"Love them," she said, and took another cookie.

I thought about all that the doctor and Mother and everyone had said about starch and fat and watched Miss Agnes happily crumbling the cookie.

"Some people," I said, "think cookies and stuff like that are unhealthy."

She brushed a crumb off her arm. "Something's going to kill me eventually, and I might as well enjoy myself until then." She gave a sigh and her chins seemed to quiver.

After that we were quiet for a while. When the potatoes were finished, Miss Alice, who hadn't said anything so far, got up, put some water in a pot, and put the potatoes in the pot and placed it on the stove over a low flame. Then she opened a big brown bag that was on the table. "Would you like to help us shell some peas?" she asked, and gave me a large handful and a bowl.

I wasn't sure how to go about it, but I watched Miss Agnes slit open a pod and slide her thumb along one side so that the peas fell out into the bowl in front of her. Then I copied her.

It was funny, I thought after a while, feeling the cool peas slide under my fingers. When two people or more were together at home, there was usually talking, or the radio or television would be on. And when I was around somebody and neither of us could think of anything to say, I felt uncomfortable. Now I didn't. I just let my mind drift, and, maybe because the peas were so green, it seemed to drift to the Green Fat Kingdom.

"Have another cookie," the Green Fat King said. He was sitting on his throne, which was made of a huge green stone. He put his hand into an enormous green burlap bag beside him, took out a cookie and held it out to the Green Fat Queen.

"Don't mind if I do," the Green Fat Queen said. Her green cloak flowed over her green throne, and emeralds sparkled in her crown.

"About Dinah," the Queen said, taking the cookie. "Did you notice that she refused the cookie when Miss Agnes offered it to her?"

"Yes," the King replied, helping himself to another cookie. "She'll never make Green Fat Princess that way. . . ."

A feeling of satisfaction stole over me and I giggled a little to myself. Miss Agnes and Miss Alice both smiled, but they didn't ask what I was giggling about.

At that point my fantasy faded into another one.

"Dinah," Dr. Brand said, "I never meant my words to have that much effect." Furtively he took out his handkerchief and wiped his eyes. "You look like a skeleton; you must put on weight."

"Darling Dinah," Mother said, "*please* have some more ice cream. . . ."

"Here's Sebastian," Miss Agnes said.

I came to with a thump. "What? Who?"

"Sebastian. My son."

I became aware of steps approaching. Then the kitchen door opened and a boy with dark hair and glasses came in, followed by Diablo and Francis. I'd expected him to be fat, too, but he wasn't. He was tall and skinny and he had a funny walk. One leg seemed to wobble around in an odd way.

"This is my son," Miss Agnes said. She sounded proud. "Sebastian Hodge. I used to call him The

Shrimp, because he was always small until quite recently. But he's growing now, aren't you, Sebastian?"

The boy nodded. Behind his glasses, his eyes seemed alert and observing.

"Now say yes," Miss Agnes said. "You know you can."

After a minute and what seemed like a small struggle, the boy said, "Yessss."

"Sebastian has a slight speech impediment," Miss Agnes explained.

"I'm sorry," I said.

"What about?"

I glanced at Sebastian, thinking it wasn't very nice to be talking about his handicap in front of him. "That he has a speech impediment."

"I d-don't mind," Sebastian said. "An-n-n—" He took a breath. "Anyway," he got out, "I'm b-better now."

"You don't go to the local school, do you?"

"I g-go to St. Monica's."

"Oh," I said. St. Monica's was a school for "special children." Local kids were sent there when they had been in some kind of bad trouble, or were handicapped in some way. Its nickname at the school I went to was the Stupid School for Backward Boobs, or, for short, the Booby Bin.

"Oh," I said, without thinking. "You go to the Boo—" And then I wished I was dead.

"The what?" Miss Agnes asked.

At that point Francis saved the situation. With a growl and a pounce he attacked Sebastian's pants leg and started pulling it. Sebastian knelt down and tickled Francis's ear. Francis rolled over, wiggling his backside.

"Would you l-like to see my animals?" Sebastian said. His stammer seemed less pronounced.

"You mean besides the cats and dogs?"

He nodded. "And p-plants."

"Yes, I'd love to."

He went through the door at the back end of the kitchen, with Francis chuffing at his heels and me following, and we came into a long, low room with one side all windows. On the other side there were wooden benches and shelves with big cages and glass tanks on them. At the rear were little wooden houses and sheds and labyrinths.

In the next half hour I met several rabbits, the gerbil family, two hamsters, two white rats, a couple of tortoises, an aquarium of fish and, when we went outside, Apollo, an ancient donkey who was peacefully plucking at the grass and weeds. The amazing thing was how tame they were. Sebastian would put a rat or a gerbil on his arm and it would run up and nuzzle his neck. Another interesting thing was his stammer: when he was talking about the animals, it almost disappeared. And the same was true when we were in the little greenhouse that ran next to the animal shed. When he talked about how he was potting some of the bulbs and moving some of the plants from small pots to larger ones, he hardly stammered at all. Also, maybe because of the evening light coming through the glass panes of the greenhouse, he didn't look so odd when he walked as he had when he'd first come lurching into the kitchen.

"You know what—" I started to say, but I never finished, because I could hear the cowbell, very faintly, across the fields. "That's my mother," I said. "It means dinner is ready. I have to go."

And then I looked down and saw Francis and my heart sank. One of the reasons I hadn't been rushing home was Francis. I knew Mother would give me a hard time.

"Don't worry," I said now to Francis. "No matter what. I'm keeping you." Then I snapped his leash back on and said good-bye and took off for home.

THREE

I'd known getting Francis past Mother would be trouble, but I hadn't realized how much. Thinking she might be in the front of the house, I went around to the back door, Francis whuffing on his leash beside me.

"Where have you been?" Mother said as I pushed through the door. Then she saw Francis. "Oh, Dinah—now what have you done?"

"His name is Francis," I said quickly. "He was going to be killed. So now he's mine."

"I really don't want any more animals in this house. You're going to have to take him back where you got him."

"I'll look after him, Mom, truly I will. You won't be bothered by him."

"And how'll you look after him when you're at school? And who housebreaks him? And what about my carpets and furniture?"

"I'll keep him in my room. Mom, you're not being fair. Tony has Brewster."

"Tony *won* Brewster for doing something well, which you don't seem able to do." She paused and bit her lip. "I didn't mean that the way it sounds. But you know you promised last year when we moved here that you'd try to pull up your grades—you really did. So did Tony, and he did pull his up, and even got the science prize. That's why we let him have Brewster. So you see, it's not being unfair." When I didn't say anything, remembering how poor my marks had been, Mother went on. "And besides, I've made arrangements for you to have counseling on food and nutrition at least two times a week, and you won't have time to take a dog for walks. So tomorrow he goes back. Where did you get him, anyway?"

I was telling her about the auction in the store when the door opened and Brenda came in.

"Hi," she said, and then she saw Francis. "What a funny-looking dog."

"Funny-looking or not," Mother said, "I've just told Dinah that he has to go back to the humane society tomorrow."

"Why?" Brenda asked. She smoothed her hair.

"Because Dinah doesn't have time to take care of him, and I don't think we need any more animals around here."

"But I told Miss Duggan that I would take one of her kittens," Brenda said.

"Come on, let's go into the dining room," Mother said. "Dinah, put your dog in the washroom. He can stay in there. And put paper down on the floor."

Francis didn't look happy when I closed the door on

him, and I heard him starting to whimper as I went into the dining room.

"Mom," I said, "please let me keep Francis. I promise you he won't be any trouble. I'll keep him in my room when I'm not here, and I'll cover up the floor with paper, but please don't make me give him back."

"Who's Francis?" Father asked.

"An unlovely mutt that Dinah brought home from town, where she was undoubtedly having ice cream, weren't you?"

"No," I lied.

But I could see from the expression on Mother's face that she knew I was lying. She had that cool, tight look that always makes my insides cringe.

"You know, Dinah," she said, "I can stand anything but your lying to me. But that's what you've been doing for weeks now, and I can't tell you how much it bothers me. All that time, whenever I've asked you where you've been in the afternoon, you've said you were in the library. And I found out you weren't. You were in the ice cream parlor every time, weren't you?"

"No," I said, this time technically telling the truth. Those previous times I hadn't been in the ice cream parlor. I'd been in my tree. And then it suddenly came to me how I might be able to save Francis. "Look. I was lying about the ice cream this afternoon. Dottie and I had some at The Spot. I won't lie again. I promise."

"And what about the lies about being in the library?"

"I was . . . was lying about that. But I wasn't in the ice cream parlor. I was—somewhere else."

"In another ice cream place, no doubt."

"Take it easy," Daddy said. "Dinah's not the prisoner at the bar."

I was crying now. Through my tears I could see Brenda sitting across from me, watching me. I decided she must know how much I hated her being there listening to what Mother was saying, and that she must be enjoying every word as she slowly ate her chicken, little bite by little bite. I knew she would leave some on her plate. She always did, and Mother always praised her. "That's right, Brenda," Mother always said. "Leave something on your plate. That way you'll never have a weight problem."

"If Francis is a puppy he'll make messes on the floor," Brenda said now.

"Who asked you?" Jack said. He had a chicken bone in one hand and gravy all over his mouth.

"Brenda's right," Mother started. "That's another reason—"

"She may be right, but her timing stinks," Daddy said. "Don't cry, Dinah. Eat your dinner."

Mother said, "I don't think it's exactly fair to blame Brenda—"

Suddenly I couldn't stand it any longer. I got up so fast I almost knocked the chair over and ran out of the room. Through the kitchen door I could hear Francis crying. When I opened the door to the washroom I saw that Brenda was right. He had done everything in the one corner of the floor where I hadn't put down paper.

"Never mind, Francis," I said. "You couldn't help it. It could happen to anybody. And I think you're beautiful."

I cleaned up the mess as fast as I could, using some

strong-smelling cleaner to wash the floor and spraying
air freshener to kill the smell. Then I put on my jacket
and took the flashlight out of one of the kitchen draw-
ers.

I'd never been up to my tree in the dark, but I felt
that I had to have some time by myself (except for
Francis, of course) to think, so I'd decided that Francis and I would go and look at the tree. I put his leash
on and took him outside.

As soon as I left the streets and started cutting
across the fields, I saw that it was actually much
lighter than I had thought it would be. For one thing,
there was a large moon; there were also a lot of stars,
and I didn't have to use the flashlight once.

All the way across, when I wasn't thinking about
what had happened at dinner, I worried about how I
was going to get Francis up the tree. Francis, not dis-
turbed by the problem at all, was either jumping from
clump to clump of grass or weeds, or stopping altogether to investigate some rich and promising smell.

"Come along, Francis," I said, impatient, and I gave
the leash a little yank. The next moment it was almost
snatched out of my hand as he hurled himself forward.

"All right, all right," I muttered to myself, and followed at a jog.

When we arrived at the tree I still hadn't figured
out how to get both Francis and me up, and the eeri-
ness of the tree at night didn't really help. But I put
the loop of the leash securely under a large rock,
shone the flashlight into the hole, got out the rule and
pulled down the rope.

"Well, Francis," I began, and then suddenly I knew
how to get him up there. I unzipped my jacket and

put Francis, leash and all, down the front, zipped it up again and tied the belt tight so he couldn't drop. Then I put the loop at the end of the leash around my wrist in case of accidents, stuck the flashlight in my pocket, and started hauling myself up the rope. Halfway up I began giggling, because Francis's muzzle was up against my chin and he was alternately blowing gently against my neck and licking it. It felt sweet and warm and affectionate, but it also tickled.

"Francis," I said, "you'll make us both fall."

Francis sneezed, blowing warm spray under my chin. Then he licked it all off.

By this time we were up on the first big fork, so I pulled myself astride and sat there, one arm around Francis, who was still cuddled against me. Then, after my eyes got accustomed to the dark up inside the leaves, I carefully climbed to the fork above, trying to keep my mind off the prospect of having to get down.

The second fork was so big and flat it was practically like a chair. I settled my fanny down on the wide part and leaned back against the trunk.

It was really beautiful—not, now, in the dark, the Green Fat Kingdom, but the Black Fat Kingdom, or maybe the Blue Velvet Fat Kingdom, with stars like diamonds and the moon like a huge round cheese shining through the leaves. If I turned my head to one side, all I saw was black with gold points; this, I realized, was the side of the hill, and the gold points were lights from the Van Hocht house. Too quickly, I tried to turn the other way to look at the lights of the village below and nearly fell out of the fork, waking Francis, who had been snoring peacefully. He wiggled and gave a yelp.

"Quiet!" I said, my hand on his head, which was in the curve of my neck. "Shh! Everything's okay."

His wiggling and quivering stopped and he started blowing on my neck again.

It was exciting in the tree at night, and I liked it. But it was also eerie. During the day when I was up here I seemed to float off into a green and gold fantasy world. But now, at night, everything was different. There was a breeze, and somewhere some practical part of me knew that after a while I would start feeling cold. I had meant to think about Mother and Brenda and what had happened at dinner, but I slipped away, instead, into a fantasy—a new one this time about the Night Fat Kingdom. I was on a spaceship, the Spaceship *Francis*, and Francis, his body warm against me, his puppy smell in my nose, was a treasure that had been given to me to guard on the journey, and he and I were on a terrific voyage of great adventure, traveling through magic casements in fairy lands forlorn. . . .

As the words drifted through my mind I knew I'd heard them before, but I couldn't remember where. Then, when they sounded in my head once or twice more, I recognized Miss Bolton's voice. Sometimes on Sundays she'd read funny things that had nothing to do with Sunday School. One day she was talking about the word "spirit," which led to something about inspiration, and she opened a book she'd brought with her and read a poem. I'd forgotten what the poem was about or who had written it, but I still could remember some of the words: "magic casements," and "fairy lands forlorn"; even a whole sentence: "I cannot see what flowers are at my feet. . . ."

I shivered a little and held Francis close and imagined the tree alone, by itself, with no houses or town near, just fields and fields of flowers below the tree, and myself walking through them blindfold. And then I remembered why that line had stuck. At the time Miss Bolton had read it, it had seemed to me tremendously sad, as though it was about somebody who was blind, feeling her way with bare feet through flowers she couldn't see. And, sitting there in the Sunday School classroom, I had started to cry.

Miss Bolton, without stopping her reading, had handed me a handkerchief. Everybody else in the class had thought I was crazy, and there'd been bursts of whispers and giggles. But when the class was over, Miss Bolton had kept me after the others left and had said, "Always remember, Dinah, how powerful words are. They can make you cry, they can make you think you're walking on air straight up to the sky, and they can make you hate yourself and wish you were dead. That's all. You can go now." I never saw Miss Bolton after that. She didn't teach Sunday School anymore. A few months later I heard that she'd died.

I hugged Francis to me and realized that now I was cold. But I didn't move, I just stared up at the moon, which seemed higher and smaller. "The moon was a ghostly galleon, tossed on something seas. . . ." Where had that come from?

Around and below me the leaves and the other trees rustled, and I heard little scamperings below. I nearly leapt off the fork when an owl screeched. Francis woke up and started yelping. He also began wiggling in an aggressive fashion, as though he really wanted to get down. After all, I realized, he didn't know he was up in a tree, and he probably wanted to go to the bathroom.

"Just a minute, Francis," I said. "Hold it!"

The prospect of Francis's not being able to hold it was such a powerful incentive that I was standing under the tree before I had plotted how to get down, and none too soon.

The moment I put Francis down he squatted in the moonlight and peed. "Good boy," I said.

After I put the foot rule away, covered up the hole and put the flashlight back in my pocket, I looked up at the Van Hocht house. There seemed to be lights in most of the windows, and I thought about Sebastian and all the dogs and cats and other animals and Miss Amelia and Miss Agnes and Miss Alice. What would happen, I wondered, if I went up there instead of going home? It seemed like a wonderful idea. But reality was reality. There'd be a terrible scene, and on the whole it was not worth it.

Francis and I went back across the fields, with Francis plunging through the grass like a miniature lion. Finally, about halfway home, he sat down suddenly, making a sort of black blob of shadow.

"What's the matter, Francis?" I asked. I leaned down and stroked him. He licked my hand and whimpered.

"Come on now," I said. "We have to go home, horrible as it is."

I started to move, but the leash pulled tight. Then Francis got up, waddled slowly forward and sat down again. It finally struck me that he must be tired, that the walk across the fields and down two streets was too much for a puppy. And besides, I remembered guiltily, he'd had no dinner. That was one of the things I'd been planning to do after dinner—feed him. I'd have done it before, except that Mother had been in the kitchen herding everybody into the dining room, so I had postponed it. And then I'd just grabbed Francis and run.

"I'm sorry, pup," I said. "Here!" I picked him up and he licked my face and I carried him back to the edge of the village.

But at the turnoff to our road I hesitated and glanced at my watch. It was a little after eight. Dinner would be over and the dishes stacked in the dishwasher. If I didn't get home right away, Mother would be angry. But she was angry anyway over my weight, and because she thought I went to the ice cream parlor every afternoon and had lied about it, and because of Francis. She would also be worried, although sometimes I did go over to Dottie's to study if we'd been given the same assignment. Then, while I was standing there, Francis started a steady whimpering. I put him down again, but he wasn't crying because he wanted to go to the bathroom. He just sat there visibly shivering, and the whimpering turned into a steady, mournful cry. I was pretty sure it was because he was hungry. After all, I knew that babies had to be fed often—at least that's what a girl in my class who has baby twin sisters once said. The same must be true of puppies, and Francis hadn't had a bite since before the auction that afternoon.

I leaned down and patted him. "I know how you feel. We'll have something right away."

At home, I thought, with Mother there telling me how he'd have to go to the humane society? And anyway, what would I feed him? I should have asked Janet Madison. And then I suddenly remembered that Mrs. Lewis lived only two blocks away. For some reason I was pretty sure she'd know what puppies should eat. And besides, I had a feeling that everything would be much better at home if we arrived back after he'd eaten. "Come on, Francis," I said. "We're going visiting."

A few minutes later I knocked on Mrs. Lewis's door.

"Hello, Dinah," she said when she opened the door. She sounded pleased. She looked down at Francis. "Who's that?"

"His name is Francis," I said.

She stepped back from the door. "You and Francis had better come in. I was just making some pies."

I knew Mrs. Lewis sometimes made pies to order. "What kind?" I asked, and breathed in. There was a delicious smell, and I suddenly felt ravenous.

"Deep dish apple and cinnamon," Mrs. Lewis said, leading the way back to the kitchen. "I just finished baking an extra to keep here at home. Want a piece?"

While she was cutting the pie, I said, "You wouldn't have any scraps or anything, would you? I haven't had a chance to feed Francis, and he's starving."

Mrs. Lewis handed me the piece of pie on a plate with a fork. "Where did you get him?"

I wanted the piece of pie so badly my mouth was watering, but I really felt I couldn't take a bite until Francis had something. Evidently Francis felt the same, because he was staring up at my plate, and a sound that was half whimper and half moan came from his throat.

While Mrs. Lewis looked in the refrigerator, I told her about the auction.

"And your mother is going to let you keep him?"

I didn't say anything. Something inside me was trying to will my mother to change her mind, and I didn't want to give out any negative vibes.

"Because Mrs. Randall is a great stickler for an orderly house," Mrs. Lewis went on, going over to the stove and putting something in a pan. "And besides—"

"Besides what?"

"Nothing. Here, I've warmed this a little. It's left-over hamburger, and I've broken up some bread with it."

I waded into the pie while Francis ate his dinner noisily and with great speed. After we were both finished I sighed. "I suppose I ought to take him out now. He's not housebroken and he's made one mess already."

Mrs. Lewis looked as though she wanted to say something but didn't think she ought to. I sat and watched Francis and felt more and more depressed. Suddenly I burst out, "Being fat makes everything so difficult. Everybody would like me better and maybe Mom would let me keep Francis if only I was thin. Brenda—" My voice felt thick and I knew I would cry if I went on, so I stopped.

"What about Brenda?" Mrs. Lewis said after a minute. She opened a drawer and handed me some tissues. "She's a sly one, that Brenda."

"You don't like her?" I said joyfully.

"I didn't say I didn't like her, though I don't. But I wouldn't trust her an inch. Not an inch."

I found this viewpoint so cheering I felt better. "Jack doesn't like her either."

"I guess, being fair to her, she's had a hard time, losing her mother and having her father go off to some outlandish place."

I wasn't particularly interested in having anyone, including Mrs. Lewis, go to such trouble to be fair to Brenda. Why were people always trying to be fair to thin people and not fat ones? It was pleasanter to think about Francis, who lay snoring on the floor in front of the big stove.

"Mother said I had to get rid of him. Do you think there's any chance she'll change her mind?"

"I wouldn't count on it, but your father might change it for her."

When I got back I found she was right. I sneaked in the back door, hoping to get upstairs before anyone saw me, but Daddy came out into the hall. "Dinah? Come in here a minute. Your mother and I want to talk to you."

I went in and found Mother sitting with her needlepoint in front of the television set and Brenda in another chair with *her* needlepoint.

"Where have you been, Dinah?" Mother said. "You know you should *never* go off like that without telling us, and particularly not slam out in that rude way before we were all finished."

There was a silence. Finally I mumbled, "I'm sorry."

"It wasn't a very nice thing to do, was it?"

"No."

Brenda looked up at me over her needlepoint, her eyes wide, her needle going up and then down. The silence got worse. I wondered if this would make Mother more determined than ever that I couldn't keep Francis. "I'm sorry," I said again. Then I added, "I was at Mrs. Lewis's." It wasn't exactly the whole truth, but it was true. Another silence. "If you don't believe me you can call her."

"The trouble with lying, Dinah," Daddy said, "is that people are inclined not to believe *anything* you say."

I didn't say anything. I still had the end of Francis's

leash in my hand, and I could hear him sitting down and scratching.

Mother took a deep breath and then said, "All right." Then she glanced down at Francis. "I can't help wishing that you had picked a more appealing and attractive animal, but . . ." She paused. "Your father and I have come to a decision. He . . . We thought that if you'd promise—*promise,* Dinah—not to eat any ice cream or other sweets for three months, we'd let you keep Francis."

I could feel my anger, like a piece of lightning inside me, jabbing away and getting bigger and bigger. I looked down at Francis. He stopped scratching and looked back at me. Then he stood up and wiggled his backside. His tail was so short it practically wasn't there; it was just a sort of comma at the end of his fat body.

So the first bite of ice cream on my part and it would be the gas chamber for Francis. *Be good, be exactly the way we want you to be, and then maybe you can have something you want.*

"Well?" Mother said. "We thought you'd be pleased."

"Okay," I said, "I'll do it."

"And the bargain includes your coming straight home from school every day. I don't want you downtown or in the village where there are ice cream parlors to tempt you. And you'll have to take care of . . . of your dog there. I won't have messes around the house."

"You mean even if I'm not going to this nutritionist and I'm not going to any ice cream place, I still have to come straight home? Like a prisoner?"

"I think Dinah has a point," Daddy said, putting

down his newspaper. "There's no need to make her feel as though she were in a reformatory."

"I'm sorry it sounded like that," Mother said. "But Dinah, I really do want you to stick with this diet so you can be like everybody else. So even though I'm not much of an animal person, I'm willing to have you keep this dog if it will help you stop your compulsive eating. And I'll make sure that there're no sweets in the place, even though it will mean penalizing the rest of the family."

"Come on," Daddy said. "You don't approve of sweets for anybody anyway."

Mother glanced at him but didn't say anything.

"Since you don't get home till around six, how will you know what I do after school?" I said. I wanted to scream, I was so angry. But I knew I couldn't because of Francis.

"Mrs. Lewis will be given strict orders to call me if you're not home after school."

I suddenly realized that one reason I was so angry was that Brenda was there. I wouldn't have minded so much if she hadn't been around to listen to Mother dressing me down. But there she sat, putting her needle into the canvas and then pulling it out again. She was sewing a flower design. I stared at it so hard it stopped looking like flowers and started looking like eggs and tomatoes spilled over everything, or maybe vomit.

"Brenda, why don't you run upstairs and get your homework done?" Daddy said suddenly.

"I've finished it, Uncle James," Brenda said. And I knew she had. She always had.

"Well, run upstairs anyway. I want to talk to Dinah."

"Sure."

I watched her slowly put all her things in her sewing carrier and slowly leave.

"Why did you send her out of the room?" Mother asked when she was gone.

"Because I don't think it's fair to Dinah to have Brenda witness your putting her down."

"I'm not—"

"Yes. You are. And what's more, you know you are."

"Well, if you think that, then I think you should have sent Dinah out of the room before you said so. I thought we were always supposed to present a united front."

"I thought so, too. But lately I've begun to think that Dinah needs a friend at court, and you often light into her when there're other people around, so I think the united front bit is canceled out."

"Why do you hate me so much?" I said to Mother. The words just popped into my head and out of my mouth before I even knew I had thought them.

"How dare you say that? I don't hate you. I love you. I love you so much I'm doing my best—with no help from you or your father—to get you to where life will be easier for you. You know what the real world's like? Fat girls don't get decent or interesting jobs. They don't get to go out much with men, and they're always looked down upon and made fun of by other people because they're fat. It may not be fair, but it's the way it is. And I don't want you to have to go through life like that just because you can't seem to control your eating. I—"

"That's enough!" Father pushed his paper onto the side table and got up. "You don't have to use a sledgehammer."

"It's you who is afraid Dinah'll never get married or have a boyfriend—you and Tony!"

"That was said in confidence, and you shouldn't repeat it now!" Father was almost shouting.

"Why not? I'm the one who's really concerned about Dinah's welfare, but the two of you together make me sound like a monster."

I was pulling Francis's leash so hard he squealed. Their quarreling was as bad as Mother's picking on me, and I was suddenly afraid I was going to be sick. "I'm going upstairs," I said, and I left.

When I got into the room and had finished creating a sort of walled-off playpen for Francis, so he wouldn't wander over to Brenda's half of the room, she put down her book and said, "Did Aunt Lorna tell you? She's going to let me have that kitten, the one out of Miss Duggan's cat's litter."

"Congratulations," I said. I knew now why Francis was staying. Even Mother didn't have the nerve to refuse to let me keep him, if she let Brenda have her cat.

The next morning when I woke up I found that Francis had made a mess on the floor in his playpen. At least he'd used the paper.

"Pee-euw!" Brenda said when she got up, and held her nose.

I didn't say anything. I was afraid that if I said what I thought, she'd tell Mother and then Mother would make me keep Francis in the basement. I took him out, and put some more paper down and squirted air freshener. I was so afraid that she would say something at breakfast that I wasn't even hungry.

Mother was always the first to leave in the morning. She belonged to a car pool that came by for her at a quarter to eight. Then the rest of us left, and after that Daddy would get in his car and drive to the city.

Today I ran over to Mrs. Lewis's. "Would you please take Francis out in the middle of the day?" I asked her. "I get a dollar a week pocket money, and I'll give you half."

"You don't have to pay me," Mrs. Lewis said. "I'll do it."

"And if he's made any messes, would you change the paper?"

"All right. But I hope he learns soon how to wait until he's outside."

School was no worse than usual. In fact, I got an A on my English paper. But after classes there was gym. I always looked forward to gym because I would see Miss Boyer, and at the same time I always dreaded it because it was usually a disaster for me. Boys and girls used to have gym separately, but our school's pretty advanced, so gym is now for both together.

As long as we were doing calisthenics it wasn't so bad. It was when we had to jump the horse and lift ourselves on the ropes that it was so awful. I could get up my tree with the aid of a rope and by putting my feet on the trunk. But I couldn't do anything with the ropes in gym.

"Heavy heavy hangs over our heads," one of the boys said.

Everybody standing around giggled.

"Gosh, I bet with that weight she'll pull her arms out of her body."

"Be quiet!" Miss Boyer said, coming over. She faced the boy who was making the remarks. "Dinah may have a weight problem. At least she doesn't have a personality problem, which is practically incurable."

"It's her own fault," the boy said sullenly. "She eats too much."

"So that makes it all right for you to be a bully? Dinah, let's go over here to the balancing bars."

I heard the boy say something under his breath as we left. The others laughed. I thought about turning around and sticking my tongue out at them but didn't. They'd probably laugh all the harder and it would make everything worse.

"He's a bully," Miss Boyer said, as we walked to the other side of the gym. "But you really should do something about losing that weight, Dinah. It's not only unattractive and a source of misery for you, it's unhealthy. . . ."

As I heard her voice go on, I thought about Francis and the A I'd gotten in composition and the Van Hochts and the Green Fat Kingdom, where I wasn't fat enough to be Green Fat Princess.

". . . so I don't know what to suggest," Miss Boyer said.

I looked at her. She looked so kind and pretty. I put my hand on her arm. She stepped back. "Now just remember what I said, won't you? Okay, everybody, come to the center of the floor here, and we'll all have a go at seeing how fast we can get over the horse." She paused. "Dinah, you're excused."

I walked by myself across the room. There was a funny noise in back of me. I turned around. Waddling with legs apart, the same boy was imitating the way I walked. As I ran out I heard Miss Boyer say, "Leonard Lambert, you can report to the principal's office right after gym."

It didn't help any to know that he'd get into trouble. It would just make him meaner.

I wanted to find out about the Van Hochts, but didn't know how to ask without letting people know that I'd been there. Since the Van Hochts were the oldest family in town, a good place to start looking, I decided, would be the library. And at least if Mother went snooping around she'd find out I'd been there.

There was a pet shop on the way to the library, so I stopped and asked the man in there what to do about Francis.

He asked, "How old is your dog?"

"About four or five months."

"Well, the best way to train him at that age is to take him out every hour or so."

"But I'm at school."

"Isn't there somebody at home who could do it for you?"

"Well . . ." I said. "Mother works." And somehow I didn't see myself asking Mrs. Lewis to take him out every hour.

"Then when you're out, the best thing to do is to keep him in one room with paper all over the floor. Better make it a room without a carpet, like a kitchen or a good-sized bathroom. He'll probably just use one corner of the room for his personal needs. Then, when you go home, you can pick up the used paper and throw it away. But be sure to keep paper in that corner, and every time he goes either on the paper in the corner or when he's out, praise him lavishly."

"I've heard you're supposed to use a rolled-up news-paper to spank puppies with if they make a mistake. But I don't like the idea of doing that, especially not to Francis."

"Neither do I. I'd rather emphasize the reward. And then when you *are* home, you can take him out often. What breed is he?"

"Mostly pug."

"Pugs are bright little dogs. He'll catch on. If it really doesn't work, then I guess you'll have to try obedience school."

"How much does it cost?"

"I dunno. About fifty dollars."

Well, I don't have fifty dollars, I thought as I walked away. And besides, I would rather train him myself. I decided to see if there were books with fur-ther suggestions on training in the library.

There were a lot of books on dog training in the library, but they mostly just repeated what the pet shop man had said. When I passed the desk on the way out, I said to Miss Laird, the librarian, "Do you know anything about the Van Hocht place? I mean, is it historic or something?"

I'd expected her to want to know why I was asking, and I had a story about a school research project on the village all worked out. What I didn't look for was her enthusiasm. Twenty minutes later I left, having learned that the Van Hochts had practically founded the place, that they had once been very rich but didn't have any money now, and that they wouldn't do anything the historical society wanted them to do to preserve their mansion. . . .

"It's a run-down monstrosity," Miss Laird said, slap-ping books around the counter. "It isn't as though we—the society—wanted them to spend any money. We have enough funds ourselves. But they won't even let us inside."

In my head I saw Miss Amelia, Miss Agnes, Miss Alice, Desmond, Sebastian and the whole big warm sloppy house with all the books and animals. "Maybe they just want to be private," I said.

Miss Laird sighed. "I guess so. And I can't blame them, I guess. Sometimes my enthusiasm for old village buildings gets out of hand." She glanced at me. "Why did you want to know?"

"No reason," I said. . . .

When I got home I found Francis in the kitchen. He flung himself at me, barking with delight. "Did he have any more accidents?" I asked.

"No," Mrs. Lewis said. "I got to him just in time and took him out. Your mother wants you to call her at work."

"Did she say why?"

"No. But she wanted to be sure you did it."

I wondered if the school or Miss Boyer had called her.

"Want a cookie?" Mrs. Lewis said. She held out a plate.

My mouth started to water and my stomach felt hollow. I made myself think about Francis.

"No," I said. "I had to promise not to eat any stuff like that so I could keep Francis." As I said that, I felt, along with the hunger and the mouth-watering, a spurt of resentment.

Mrs. Lewis didn't say anything. I looked at her. "Does it bother you when people tell you you're—" I paused, not wanting to offend her. Especially since she was helping me with Francis.

"That I'm fat?" Mrs. Lewis said. "I tell 'em to go fly a kite. You should too." She looked at me. "I like fat little girls."

"Oh," I said, wondering why I didn't feel a boost in my morale.

"It's too bad about your promise to your mother. I made these cookies especially for you." She reached out with her pudgy hand and patted my arm. Her hand felt damp. I pulled my arm away, and then I remembered Miss Boyer pulling her arm away.

"I'll go call Mother," I said.

Mother said, "I want you to go to the square and get the next bus that goes to the north side of town and up into the country. It should leave in about twenty minutes. You can catch it if you hurry."

"Why do I have to go there?"

"I'm about to tell you, if you'll just let me finish. The bus will drop you off near St. Monica's School, and—"

"St. Monica's!" I almost shouted. "That's the Booby Bin!" And then I remembered Sebastian Hodge.

"It's not a booby bin," Mother said. "It's a special school for children who have problems."

"Mom, I don't want to go there. If anybody found out, they'd think—"

"They'd think what, Dinah? That you have a problem? Don't you think they think that anyway?"

I couldn't find anything to say.

"Now listen here," Mother went on. "Your father and I are allowing you to keep Francis. The least you can do is to cooperate about your weight problem. Sister Elizabeth—"

"A nun?"

"Yes. She happens also to be the best nutritionist in this part of the state, and she works with people who have weight problems."

"Mom, don't make me go. They sound like freaks. I'm not a freak."

Silence. Then: "You promised you would cooperate with us in our effort to—"

"I said I wouldn't eat any ice cream or candy or anything like that."

"Your promise to help us help you was implicit in that. Now if you want me to accept having an extra, unhousebroken animal around the house—"

"You mean if I won't go, you'll take Francis away?"

Pause. Then Mother said, "Yes, I will."

I looked down at Francis, who was sniffing around the floor. I wondered if he was about to have an unhousebroken accident. Then he raised his head and looked at me.

"All right," I said. "I'll catch the bus." Then I hung up before she could say anything else.

"Come on, Francis," I said. "Let's go to the Booby Bin."

FOUR

I don't know what I'd expected of St. Monica's—
something that looked like a factory with bars, I
guess. Instead, it turned out to be a large red brick
house with a couple of phony towers, a porch, and a
big lawn.

A short elderly nun dressed in a long black robe
opened the door.

"I've come to see Sister Elizabeth," I said.

"And your name is?"

"Dinah Randall."

The nun looked down at Francis. The bus driver
hadn't been too happy about having him on the bus,
and the nun seemed a little doubtful.

"Is he trained?" she asked.

"Yes," I said, and crossed my fingers.

"You may wait in the hall here," the nun said, and
she walked through a door at the back of the hall.

I sat there, with Francis sitting on my feet, trying to
imagine what Sister Elizabeth would be like. I was

pretty sure I knew: short, fat, with a weight problem she was trying to overcome through prayer. "Yuch!" I said to myself.

Francis got off my feet, waggled his backside, then tried to jump on my lap. I pulled him up on my knees. I knew now why Mother wanted me to see Sister Elizabeth: she and Daddy had probably decided that since no man would ever look at me, and I'd never have a boyfriend, the best thing for me to do was to become a nun.

I was staring down at the floor, and saw the black robe and the dowdy black laced shoes come back.

"Dinah Randall?" a different voice said.

I looked up. Even in that terrible outfit she was one of the most beautiful women I'd ever seen in my life. She was tall, and her eyes were as blue as the sea under the sun as I had seen it one summer vacation, and her eyelids curled upwards at the outer edges. She was looking down at me and smiling, and I blurted out, "What color is your hair?"

"Brown. I'm Sister Elizabeth. You're Dinah, aren't you?"

"Yes." I got up, spilling Francis onto the floor. Suddenly he started sniffing and I saw his backside begin to go down.

"No!" I yelled. Snatching him up, I tore across the hall, opened the door and ran down the steps. Then I put him down on the gravel drive, where he immediately lowered his backside and peed.

"He's not quite housebroken," I said to Sister Elizabeth, who was standing on the top step. I wondered if the other nun had told her about my lie about Francis's being housebroken.

"He'll learn," Sister Elizabeth said. "But I think

we'd better put some newspaper down in my office. Come along."

I wondered if she would tell Mother, and if Mother would try to make me get rid of Francis. Well, I thought, following Sister Elizabeth through the door at the back of the hall, if Mother could blackmail me, I could blackmail her by promising that I would eat every sundae in sight if she took Francis away. But then she'd probably lock me in my room. And where would it get me, besides fatter? A feeling of depression settled down over me.

"Now," Sister Elizabeth said, going into a small room looking out over the back of the house, "let's put some of this newspaper down." And she picked up several sections of the Sunday paper. While she was doing that, I went over to the windows and looked out. There were a few adults—some of them nuns—and a lot of kids of various ages outside. Some of them were fat, much fatter than me; others seemed disabled in one way or another; a few were in wheelchairs and others looked as though they might be retarded. As I watched, I was overwhelmed by a terrible feeling that Mother was just breaking me in slowly, that soon she and Daddy would take me out of the local school I was in and would send me here, where I'd be one more freak among all the other freaks. And everybody would know. And it was all more horrible than I could bear.

I started crying then, and I couldn't stop. I knew I was making a noise and being a baby, but none of it mattered. I was sure Sister Elizabeth would pat my shoulder or hand me some tissues, or tell me to stop crying, or do something obvious, and I waited for it. But time passed and finally my crying fit seemed to run out of steam. I groped around in my bag and in my pocket for some tissues. I felt swollen all over, and my nose was stopped up. I looked over at the nun. She and Francis were having a quiet game with a small rubber ball.

"Do you have any tissues?" I asked finally, feeling that she might have asked me first.

"In the bathroom over there." Sister Elizabeth nodded in the direction of another door.

I went into a small bathroom, pulled a handful of tissues out of a box, washed my face with cold water and then dried it, and then went back into the other room.

"Feel better?" Sister Elizabeth asked.

"Yes," I said grudgingly.

"You hate being here," she said. It was a statement, not a question. "You hate the fact that your mother sent you here because you're afraid it makes you like everyone else here. Isn't that about it?"

On the nose, I thought. But I just nodded.

"Well," she said, "I understand, and I don't altogether blame you, but that's not helping you solve your problem, is it? Are you learning how to housebreak this puppy? What's his name, by the way?"

"Francis. Yes. At least the man in the pet shop says to put down paper and when I'm home to take him out every hour. And when he does something right to praise him."

"That's right, and you can say 'no' in a severe voice when he makes a mistake. Animals learn to understand that no means no. Of course, you have to make sure he knows, whether he's made a mistake or not, how wonderful you think he is."

"Everybody says he's ugly. I don't think he's ugly. I think he's beautiful."

"Of course he is. But do you care? I mean, do you care whether he's everyone's idea of beautiful or not? He's himself. That's what you love, isn't it?"

"Yes," I said. "That's it exactly." And I reached out and rubbed him between the ears and he waggled his whole backside with pleasure.

"You see. He wants to please you. That is his big priority. So the whole thing is just to let him know how to do that." She got up and took a book from a bookshelf near her desk. "I have a book here, written by one of our former students, on living with a dog or puppy. She's now a vet for one of the biggest humane societies in New York and talks on radio and television about animals. I'll lend you the book. It's the only copy we have, so I know you'll bring it back."

I looked in the book, and we started talking about it.

"We have lots of animals here," Sister Elizabeth said after a while. "They're under the general care of Sebastian."

I looked up. "Sebastian Hodge?" And then I added without thinking, "His mother says she used to call him The Shrimp."

Sister Elizabeth smiled. "That's right. But I think he likes being called now by his real name best. What does your mother call you?"

"Fat," I said. "She doesn't actually call me fatso, but she might as well." I paused. "What does Sebastian do with the animals here?"

"Looks after them. He's very good with them. If some of the kids have been making a noise and the hamsters and gerbils are all excited and upset, Sebastian walks in and they just calm down like that. It's astounding." Sister Elizabeth reached over to the shelf again and pulled a thin book, a sort of pamphlet, off a pile of others. "I'm going to give you another book—a very small one. It's about different kinds of foods and what they do for your body."

"You mean proteins and fats and that kind of thing?"

"So you know about them."

"Dr. Brand talks about them sometimes. Proteins are good, fats are bad and carbohydrates are worst of all."

Sister Elizabeth smiled. "Not quite. You couldn't stay alive and healthy without eating all three. They all play a part. It's in what proportion and how much that counts." She looked at me. "Will you read the book for me?" She handed me the book and consulted a plain silver watch hanging by its strap from a rope thing around her waist. "It's time you caught the bus back," she said. "I'll see you Tuesday.

"By the way," she said, walking along the corridor with me to the front hall, "I think you're right about Francis. He is quite beautiful."

"You really think that? You're not just saying it?"

"I really think it. I wouldn't say it if I didn't."

I don't know why that made me feel so much better. It had nothing to do with fat. "I'll see you Tuesday," I said.

The bus let Francis and me off at the foot of the hill. When we got to the road leading off to the fields and the tree, I stopped and looked at my watch. Dinner was about half an hour away. There really wasn't time to get across the fields and up the tree, and I didn't have on my jacket, so I wouldn't be able to take

Francis up with me. But by this time I was walking rapidly down the street towards the fields. "Just this once, Francis, you'll have to wait at the bottom," I said. "I promise I won't be up there long."

Francis responded by hurtling off towards some bushes into which a small tiger cat was disappearing. There was a slight hissing noise and a yelp.

"That'll teach you to be aggressive with cats," I said, as I got out a tissue and wiped the blood off his nose. "And you might as well learn it now, if Beastly Brenda is going to have one." Francis gave a faint, disheartened wag of his behind.

I was so pleased with "Beastly Brenda" that I said it to myself all the way across the fields. "*Beastly* Brenda," I said, and then I tried, "Beastly *Brenda*. Which do you like better?" I asked Francis.

"Wuff!" he said, and attacked one of my sneakers.

When we got to the tree, I said, "Why don't you take a short nap now? I'll just put a rock on your leash." And I did so.

As I hauled myself up, I was glad that he seemed more interested in digging around the roots, especially under the rock where I kept my foot rule, than in being up in the tree with me. But after I got up, I found that I couldn't just sit down in my upper fork in the Green Kingdom and forget all about Francis. I sat in the lower fork where I could keep an eye on him and looked up into the tree so that I was half in and half out of the Green Kingdom.

Somehow my mind wouldn't soar and take off into my fantasy, but kept worrying about Francis. It was all very frustrating for me, and it was not an arrangement that Francis liked. He tugged and whined and would make sudden runs towards the tree and me, only to be stopped short by the taut leash hauling him back on his hind legs.

"I'll be down in a minute," I said.

He sat down and cried.

I sighed and came down and we headed back across the fields.

I slid into my seat at the dining table as inconspicuously as possible, praying that Mother wouldn't say, "How was St. Monica's?" so that everyone, meaning Brenda and Tony, would know I'd been to the Booby Bin.

Instead, Mother looked at me and smiled. "Hi," she said. "Have a good day?"

"Fine, thanks."

Daddy put some roast beef on my plate. "What was so special about today?" He handed my plate to Mother, who gave me some carrots and string beans and, after a fraction of a second of hesitation, a baked potato.

There was the problem again. How could I answer his question without giving everything away?

"I gave Dinah a private assignment and I was just inquiring about it, that's all," Mother said.

I looked at Brenda, who had put a tiny bite of roast beef into her mouth and was slowly chewing it.

"How's Francis?" Jack said.

"He's fine."

"I have a kitten," Brenda said.

"Where?"

"He's upstairs in my room."

"It's Dinah's room, too," Jack said belligerently.

Brenda opened her eyes a little wider so that you could see all the round colored part, like a brown marble with a black middle. "I know." She looked at me. "Do you mind me saying 'my room'? I mean, since Aunt Lorna said she wanted me to feel like this was my home . . ." Her voice trailed off. Her eyes grew a little wet.

"Of course it's your home, Brenda," Mother said. "And of course Dinah doesn't mind your saying 'my room.' I know she wants you to feel that this is your home as much as I do. Don't you, Dinah?"

I swallowed the last of the potato skin, which is my favorite part of the potato. "Sure." Without thinking too much about it, I reached out for another potato.

"No," Mother said. "I don't want you to have another, Dinah. Didn't the nutritionist at St. Monica's—"

"St. Monica's?" Tony said.

"Isn't St. Monica's the school for kids who are retarded and handicapped? I know they have nuns up there," Brenda said.

"Yes," I said. "It's the Booby Bin, where I belong. Are you planning to send me there full time, Mother?"

"No. Of course not. I'm just sending you up there to see the nutritionist. And don't use that term, 'booby bin.' It's a put-down of all the people there. They may have problems, but they deserve to be talked about as though they were people, like the rest of us."

I knew Brenda would never actually gallop around me screaming, "Dinah's going to the Booby Bin." But some of her friends might. By tomorrow it would be all over the school.

"What's your cat named?" I asked her.

"Jupiter."

"Why Jupiter?"

"Because he was the top god, and I think my cat is going to be, too."

"Unless he turns out to be a goddess," Daddy said.

"Can't you tell?" Jack asked.

"It's a little difficult," Mother said. "When he—or she—is older, it'll be easier."

"I'm sure it's a boy," Brenda said.

I said a prayer that it would be a girl.

"Well, Dinah, now that one cat is out of the bag, no pun intended," Mother said, "how do you like Sister Elizabeth?"

"She's okay," I replied. I was very angry about Mother's slip.

"Does she wear slacks or a miniskirt the way modern nuns do?" Daddy asked.

"That's a pretty prejudiced comment," Mother said.

"No it's not. They do. I've seen pictures of them. And there's that big convent that one of my partner's daughters goes to. He says they all wear pants suits."

"He probably wishes women never got the vote," Mother said.

"Speaking of prejudice," Daddy commented, grinning.

"She wears a long black dress with old-fashioned black laced shoes and a sort of veil thing." I tried to show how it looked with my hands. "And across her forehead is a white thing."

"Wimple," Mother said. "I think that particular order voted not to change their habit."

"I think it's funny that she should be such an expert in something like nutrition and be so old-fashioned in other ways," Brenda said.

When we got upstairs, I pushed Brenda down on her bed. "If you tell a soul at school that I'm going to St. Monica's, I'll . . . I'll make you sorry."

"How?" Brenda was lying on her back on the bed. She should have been the underdog, but she wasn't.

"Don't worry. I'll think of a way. I'll take Jupiter outside and let him get lost." The minute I said it, I knew how wrong it was. How would I feel if it was Francis? "No, I won't do that. But I'll think of something. Where is he?"

Brenda got up and rubbed her wrists. "Under the bed. And there's no way you can stop me saying anything I want to say."

"Oh, isn't there! You'll find out!" Which was pretty funny. Because I didn't know what I would do. Then I went downstairs to find Francis.

As I was about to take him out for a walk, Mother came into the kitchen. "I'm sorry I mentioned the nutritionist in front of Brenda," she said. "It wasn't very sensitive of me. I just wasn't thinking. But I do want to know how you and she got on, and what you talked about."

"We talked about . . . about fats and protein and stuff," I said. I was about to say we'd discussed Francis much more than we'd discussed food, but I was afraid that Mother would be annoyed at that and not let me go back. I was surprised to find that I was looking forward to my next visit.

"What did she say about your weight?"

"Nothing."

"Maybe she likes fat little girls the way I do," Mrs. Lewis said. She was feeding dishes into the dishwasher.

Mother opened her mouth. "I'm not—" she started to say.

But I was overcome by the feeling that if I didn't get out before she finished that sentence, I'd be very sorry. "I have to take Francis out," I said. "I'll be back later."

While I was watching Francis sniff around the weeds and bushes, I thought about Mrs. Lewis's saying "I like fat little girls." She'd said it twice now. The funny part was that it turned me off even though I'd often fantasized about how somebody else—like Mother or a really cool handsome boy—would say the same thing. When Mrs. Lewis said it, I felt she wanted something in return; I felt as though she were trying to buy me or make me love her or something.

When I came back into the house, Mrs. Lewis had gone. I was about to go upstairs with Francis when he caught sight of Brewster across the hall in the living room with Mother and Daddy. Brewster was asleep on the hearthrug.

"Francis, come back," I yelled. But it was too late. Francis went down on his front paws with his behind in the air. Then he said, "RRRRRRRuuuffff!" and charged straight at Brewster's tail.

Brewster is a quiet dog with nice manners. But he was sound asleep when Francis launched his assault. He gave a wild yelp and leapt into the air. Francis was beside himself with delight. He made another charge and then hurled himself around an end table, which rocked and crashed to the floor.

"Oh no!" Mother yelled. She sprang from her chair. "Why did it have to be my favorite piece of Royal Doulton?" She picked up the shepherd's broken head from the carpet. "Dinah, I don't mean to lean on you. I truly don't. But I think maybe you'd better keep Francis out of the living room until he grows up a little. I'm going to take this out to the kitchen and see if that new glue is as good as its advertising says it is."

"And upstairs Brenda has a kitten who'll probably scratch Francis," I said bitterly to Daddy, when Mother had left.

"Then I think you and Brenda should devise some means of dividing the room," Daddy said. "Francis is entitled to his space. Aren't you, boy?" And he leaned down and patted Francis on the head. Francis's ears went down. His backside wagged. His eyes seemed almost to bulge with affection. "He's an appealing little thing," Daddy said. "Even though he is so ugly."

"He's not ugly."

Daddy straightened and glanced at me. "I take it back. He's not ugly. And anyway, there's an old saying, handsome is as handsome does."

I thought that over as I squatted down beside Francis and stroked his ears. "I like that saying," I said. "I haven't heard it before. I guess it isn't said much now. Did they used to say it when you were little?"

Daddy laughed and leaned his head back against the back of his chair. "No. I'm not that old. That was fashionable in my parents' and grandparents' day. Back then, or so I gathered from my grandmother and from some of the books she had in her house, it was important to believe, or pretend to believe, that looks didn't count, or at least that they didn't count as much as character."

"I wish I'd lived then."

Daddy leaned forward. "Baby," he said, which he sometimes calls me even though Jack is younger than me, "I wish—" Then he stopped.

"You wish what?" I said.

"I wish this thing didn't loom so large in your life. I wish you could just enjoy yourself and forget about it."

For a minute I felt wonderful. Then I remembered what Mother had said. "But you told Mom that you were afraid I'd never get married or even have a boy-friend because I'm—because of my weight. So you don't really believe that bit about character being more important."

He hesitated. "I guess I put it rather strongly. But honey, there is a germ of truth there. A nice figure certainly doesn't necessarily mean a nice person, but there's no question but that a girl with a slim shape has a powerful advantage. Usually a boy sees that before he sees anything else." He paused again. "Your mother would say that's a sexist comment. Which it probably is, but it's also true."

It was funny. Daddy's voice was kind, and I knew that he loved me. But knowing that didn't help any. And I felt worse than I'd felt about anything Mother had said. For a minute a crazy scene played itself in my head: there I was at the gate of heaven, asking to be let in.

"No," said God. "I'm sorry and it's too bad, but it's the law. No fat person in heaven."

I stared down at the floor where Francis had gone, quite suddenly, to sleep, in the way he had. Brewster, who had recovered from the attack on his tail, was lying in front of the fireplace with his long black nose between his black paws.

Daddy leaned forward. "Don't feel bad, sweetheart. I know you can lose weight if you just put your mind to it. Maybe Sister Elizabeth will help."

I heard steps and saw Brewster's head come up.

"Dinah?" Daddy said. "Did you hear me?"

"Yes," I said.

"Come sit on my lap. I'm beginning to feel like

Frankenstein's monster. Now come on, or I'll feel un-loved."

I'd always liked to sit on Daddy's lap when I was younger, though I hadn't done much of it lately. But it seemed like a good idea. I got up. Daddy straightened and put his knees together. Gently I lowered myself onto them.

"Crunch!" Tony's voice said from the doorway.

"That's neither kind nor intelligent," Daddy said. "You have your own faults."

Tony grinned. "But they don't show." He walked in in his sweat shirt and running shoes. Tony's a terrific runner and wants to run in the Boston Marathon.

"Oh yes they do," Daddy said. "Dumbness combined with a swelled head can be powerfully unattractive."

I could see from his face that Tony didn't like that. "All Dinah has to do is stop stuffing herself and take some exercise. C'mon, Brewster, let's go for a walk."

At that moment something happened that made me feel very good. Jack walked in. Brewster, who had just looked up for Tony, got to his feet and loped over to Jack and tried to lick his face.

"Brewster's got taste," I said. "He prefers Jack."

"Yeah? Well, he's my dog, and he's coming out for a walk with me." Tony put his hand inside Brewster's collar and tugged.

"Hey, take it easy," Jack said. "That hurts him. How'd you like somebody to haul you around by your collar?"

"Just letting him know who owns him," Tony said. "Now sit. Sit!" Brewster, who had been obedience trained, sat down. But he looked towards Jack.

"He knows who owns him, maybe," I said. "But he also knows who he likes best, and it's Jack."

"Who asked you, fatty?"

Daddy stood up, pushing me off. "You'll apologize for that, Tony. Now."

Tony is almost as tall as Daddy, and they look a lot alike. "Well, if it'd make her stop gorging—"

"You'll apologize. Right now," Daddy said. He stood there with his hands in his pockets and his nose thrust forward.

"Okay. I apologize. But maybe I'd like to feel proud of her for a change. Why can't she be like Brenda?"

"Because she's a lot nicer than Brenda!" Jack shouted. "Brenda's a creep!"

"Who said that?" Mother said, coming back into the room. She was holding the shepherd, who now had his head on. "Jack, was that you? How could you shout like that? She might hear you, and it's our job to make her feel at home."

"Let me handle this, Lorna," Daddy said.

"Well, I don't think that letting Jack get away with—"

"I was here from the beginning of this, and you weren't. Now just let me finish."

Mother closed her mouth tight. "All right," she said finally.

"You sure took that lying down," Tony said.

Daddy turned towards him. "Tony," he said in a calmer voice, "you and I are going to go outside and talk."

"I have to go—"

"Immediately," Daddy said, and took his arm.

But they didn't make it. The center of attention shifted to Francis, who had quietly, and unnoticed until that moment, been making a large puddle in the corner on the carpet.

Half an hour later I was upstairs on my bed, holding Francis and waiting for some kind of axe to fall. Mother had been so stunned when she'd seen what Francis had done that she'd just stood there, frozen. So I'd managed to get Francis out of there in the general noise and confusion of Tony laughing, and Jack yelling at Tony, and Daddy saying very quietly, twice, "Oh my God! Oh my God!" And then, in a despairing sort of tone: "*Now* what are we going to do?"

I'd just picked up Francis and run as fast as I could up the stairs and into my room. . . .

Brenda was there, playing with her ginger cat, Jupiter.

She must have read something on my face. "What'd he do?" she asked. "Have an accident?"

I put Francis down on the bed and lay down beside him, with my arm over him. I felt, somehow, that he was terribly threatened. "Yes." I was too unhappy to care whether or not she knew.

"Too bad a dog isn't like a cat," she said. "Jupiter is so good about his pan."

"I want to be alone," I said.

"It's my room, too."

"I don't care. I want to be alone for a while. Can't you go downstairs just for a bit?"

"You're not making me feel at home," Brenda said.

"I'm sorry. But I want to be alone."

Finally, she went. "I'll leave Jupiter in the bathroom," she said.

I could hear him scratching around after she'd left.

I would never, never admit it to her, but she was right that it was too bad dogs didn't use litter pans. "Never mind, Francis," I said. "Everything's going to work out."

I wanted to be alone because I felt miserable. But there was another reason. At the bottom of my laundry bag, hanging in my closet, were a package of chocolate-chip cookies and two candy bars. The bag was the only place I could be sure neither Mother nor Brenda would go snooping into. I think Mother thought that nobody, not even I, would put food in a dirty-clothes bag. So therefore it was safe, and I was having a terrible attack of the hungries, the worst I had had in days.

I suddenly realized I'd been thinking about the candy bars ever since I'd sat on Daddy's lap and Tony had said, "Crunch!" Crunch had made me think of Chocolate Crunch. If Brenda went downstairs for even a minute, I'd have time to eat one candy bar. I'd once seen Mother pick up sewing pins off the floor with a steel magnet, and I felt now as though I was a pin and the candy bars were a magnet—as though, almost, I didn't have any will or choice of my own. I sat up. Then the door opened and Daddy came in.

"Things were a little hairy there for a while. But I managed to save Francis's bacon by reminding your mother that you promised, if you could keep him, that you wouldn't eat any sweets. Right?"

The candy bar in my mind seemed as big as an airplane. "Right," I said, mentally pushing it back.

"Okay. So keep your part of the bargain, won't you? Your mother was very fond of that carpet, and I'm not at all sure that the stain will come out. But I promised her that I'd have an expensive, professional cleaner have a go at it. Couldn't you get busy and train Francis?"

"I should have made sure he went when I took him out," I said. "I'll remember after this, truly. And if I can't take him out practically every half hour, I'll put him in my bathroom, or the one downstairs, with some paper."

"Well, I've gone out on a limb for you. The rest— your promise and training Francis—is up to you. Okay?"

"All right." I let my mind drift back to the candy bar.

Daddy looked around the room. "If anyone seeing this room thought one person lived here, there'd be an instant diagnosis of severe schizophrenia. I take it yours is the chaotic half?"

I nodded and looked at my open desk, practically invisible under books, papers, two bags of Fritos that I'd forgotten about, a pair of tights and my old sneakers. All over my half of the floor were more shoes, socks and a couple of T-shirts. My bed was made up, but only because Mother stood over me in the morning to make me do it. Right down the middle of the room everything changed. Brenda's bed was made, Brenda's desk had nothing on it except a lamp and Brenda's half of the closet looked like a rack in a store.

From the bathroom came loud, sad meowing. I felt sorry for Jupiter, who was an animal and therefore nice, even though he belonged to Beastly Brenda.

"Beastly Brenda," I said aloud.

Daddy looked at me. "I know what you mean. But I guess it's not really any more her fault that she's the way she is than it's your fault that you're the way you are. Which sounds like the ultimate cop-out for anything anybody wants to do, and I don't mean it that way."

"What do you mean about Brenda?"

Daddy put his hands in his pockets, then strolled around the room looking at the posters and pictures on the walls. "She didn't have the greatest possible home life, you know. Maybe she feels now that only if she obeys all the rules and does everything just right and calls your attention to it all the time can she avert some calamity."

"She thinks that? That's crazy!"

"On some level. Not consciously, probably. Anyway, it's just a guess. I'm an engineer, not a psychologist. But she does powerfully remind me of a guy I used to work with who was always rushing up to the boss trying to make points one way or another."

"Mother likes her better than me. She hates me because I'm . . . I'm fat. Nothing I do is right."

I'd never come right out and said anything like this to Daddy before, or even talked to him—just the two of us—that much before, and I wouldn't have now if I hadn't been so miserable. For a minute I held my breath, not knowing what he was going to do. He frowned, and I wished I hadn't said anything. Then he sat down on the bed. "I have a feeling you ought to be saying this to your mother." He paused, hoping, I guess, that I'd agree. When I didn't, he sighed. "If she knew you thought this way she'd be horrified. And it's not true. She loves you—"

"No, she doesn't."

"Yes, she does."

"N—"

"And I won't have you talking that way." He said it with a snap.

I didn't reply.

"Or thinking it," he added.

I sat on the side of the bed and stared at my toes.

"Listen," Daddy said. "You're wrong."

"She didn't want me even to be born. She told me so."

"That's not true, either, Dinah. Or at least not the way you're making it sound. You've distorted everything."

"That's what she told me," I said.

"Is it? I find that hard to believe—that she'd actually say that."

Daddy's gray eyes, the color of clouds, seemed to bore into me. I could almost feel myself squirming. "Well . . . she said I was a surprise."

"That's not quite the same, is it? And that's what I mean about distorting." He paused and said in a voice that wasn't as tight or angry-sounding, "It's true you were a surprise. Very unexpected."

"Didn't you use birth control?"

I looked up and was startled to see that his cheeks were red.

"I suppose you know all about birth control," he said.

"Sure."

"Well, then, you might as well know that it doesn't . . . always . . . work. And," he said as I opened my mouth, "I do not intend to go into the whys and wherefores. Just take my word for it. Anyway, we were going on a new assignment into the wilds of Central America. Tony and Donald were with your grandmother, and your mother was going to use that year to get back into the kind of economics journalism that was her specialty. She had collected assignments to write pieces for some of the better financial and political magazines. And she was very up about the whole thing, because she was convinced that the way things were working out, it went to prove that she could be a mother *and* have a career. And then one day when she and I were in a Jeep in Guatemala on our way to Lake Atitlán, in the mountains, she got sick. And she was sick the next day and the next. When we got back down to Guatemala City and went to a doctor, he shook her hand and congratulated her all over the place and told her she was pregnant." Daddy laughed suddenly. I had a feeling he'd almost forgotten it was me he was talking to. "If he'd told her that she'd gotten some particularly horrible tropical disease she couldn't have been more shattered—and she might have been a lot less angry. She—"

He stopped and stared at me; then he leaned over and took my hand. "Listen, sweetheart, we both love you and are delighted you're here. It's just . . . you know your mother, honey. She likes to deal in five-year plans, and this one really got shot to pieces. If it's any consolation to you, she was mad at me, too, for—er—my share in the whole thing. Anyway, maybe she would have calmed down if it had been an easy pregnancy like the other two—"

"She told me. She said all the others were okay, but when she was pregnant with me it was awful. Do you think it's because I'm the only girl?"

"I don't see why that would make it different."

"Maybe it's because she really didn't want me."

"I wondered about that." Daddy sounded as though

he were talking to himself. He muttered, "I just don't know."

"Maybe it's because I was fat." I shoved the word out, angry at him and at Mother and myself.

"But you weren't. You were late and rather large. But you weren't fat. That came later."

"When?"

"You were fine till we went off to India, leaving you with Granny, when you were five. When we got back a year later you'd put on a lot of weight. But then when we took you back abroad with us, you put on more."

"You left Jack with Granny sometimes. He didn't get fat."

"Sometimes people seem to be born with dispositions that nothing upsets. Or maybe he was upset but didn't show it. Maybe he'll go on not showing it and everybody will think he's fine till he grows up and all of a sudden goes around murdering all women—or men—over forty." Daddy sighed. "Who knows?" He glanced at me. "Joke," he said. "Don't take that seriously. Now, honey, keep your part of the promise, won't you?" He patted Francis's behind. "He's a nice dog and I want you to keep him."

Francis opened his eyes, sneezed, and licked Daddy's hand.

FIVE

After Daddy left I sat on the bed and thought about what he'd said. Having him confirm the fact that Mother hadn't wanted me in the first place didn't make me feel any better. And then there was my promise.

"Well, that's it," I said to Francis. "No sweets—no candy bars, no cookies, no ice cream." I thought about my secret hoard at the bottom of the laundry bag. Somehow, just having them there, knowing they were there, made me feel better, safer. "Why don't I just leave them there?" I said aloud to Francis. "They aren't doing any harm."

"Leave what there?" Brenda asked, coming in. "What's not doing any harm?"

I stared at her.

She said, "I'd better see if Jupiter's all right." She opened the bathroom door and a yellow shape shot across the room towards Francis and me.

"You're a good cat, Jupiter," Brenda said. "Using your litter box like that! Good boy!"

Jupiter, who really was very handsome, came up to Francis, sniffed and then spat. Francis rose. I snatched him up. "Brenda," I said, "Mother wants to see you in the kitchen."

"I've just seen her."

"She wants to see you again."

"No, she doesn't. You're just trying to get me out of *my* room. It's my room as much as yours, and you're not making me feel a bit welcome." She paused and looked at me. Her eyes grew wider. "I bet you want me out so you can get some of those candy bars or cookies out of that dirty old laundry bag, the way you do in the middle of the night sometimes."

I could feel the blood rushing to my face. "I do *not*," I said.

"Yes, you do. Want me to go over and show you? There's probably candy there right now."

"No," I said. "I think you're loathsome."

"Better than being fat."

I went down the hall and knocked on Jack's door.

"You can't come in," he yelled. "I'm getting undressed."

"Well, hurry up."

Mother came up the stairs. All of a sudden I remembered the puddle Francis had made. She and I stood and looked at each other. "I'm sorry, Mom," I said after a minute. "About . . . about Francis. I'll really try to housebreak him."

Mother took a deep breath. "A promise is a promise is a promise," she said. "You tend to your half and I'll stick to mine."

"Yes, I will, truly," I said. The candy bar sailing

around and around in my head was now as big as one
of those huge blimps advertising tires. But it had
turned and was going away. I could see its chocolate-
peanut fins disappearing.

"What's the matter?" Mother said.

"Nothing."

"Then what are you doing out here?"

At that point Jack yelled, "Okay. You can come in
now."

"What do you want to go into Jack's room for?"
Mother asked. She glanced at her watch. "It's time,
anyway, you were getting to bed." She glanced down
at Francis, who was sniffing under Jack's door. "Better take him out again. Then take your bath and go to
bed."

"Mom—"

"Yes?" When I didn't go on, she looked at me hard.
"What is it, Dinah?"

"Could I have the room in the attic as my room? I
know there's a bed there."

"Dinah, I think there're a couple of shingles missing, and they're missing off the roof above that room.
Your father and I are planning to have the roof fixed,
but until we do, it's cold and it can be wet in the
attic."

"I don't care if it's cold, Mom. I'd just like to have a
room of my own." Maybe if I'd stopped there she
would have let me have the attic room. But Ms. Big-
mouth had to go and spoil it by saying, "The way I
used to before Brenda came."

And Mother's face, which had been opening up,
seemed to close, like a door shutting. "Dinah, Brenda
has gone through an awful lot. She lost her mother,
and she can't be with her father."

"Maybe he's trying to get away from her," I said, knowing I was destroying my last chance of getting a room to myself, but thinking, What does it matter now?

"That's not a very kind thing to say."

"Why should I be kind? People aren't kind to me."

"What do you mean by that?"

I didn't say anything. I kept my eyes on Francis, who had discovered something under his collar and was busy scratching it. Mother looked at me a little sadly. "If you mean what I think you mean about my trying to help you to moderate your eating habits, then, surely, Dinah, you must know I'm doing it for you. How on earth could I benefit from it?"

I stared at the floor and still didn't say anything.

"I wish you'd get that straight. Riding you about food is for *you*. Not me."

Silence.

Mother let out her breath. "Well, anyway, what were we talking about? Oh—the attic." She looked at me. "You see, it wasn't just a question of space; I thought Brenda would be a nice friend for you to have. Moving around as much as we have hasn't made it easy for any of you to make real friends. But I think you've suffered most of all." She sighed.

"You mean it's been harder for me than for Jack and Tony and Donald?"

"Jack came after most of the traveling. And the other two, well—for one thing they were boys, and your father would take them along with him when he had to camp out in some really remote places. And then they were close in age and had each other. And when they did go to various schools they were popular. . . ." Her voice trailed off.

yellow flower as tall as a pine, its round gold closed cup slanted down towards me as I stood underneath. But I was miserable, because inside me was a great black monster-shaped space, growing bigger every minute. Nothing will ever fill it, I thought. Soon it will eat me up from the inside out. At that moment the gold cup opened wide and light spilled everywhere, falling down over me and into me until the black space inside me was filled and overflowing with light. And I started to laugh, not because anything was funny, but because I was so happy I couldn't help it.

I went on laughing and laughing, knowing I was dreaming, even though the gold light pouring out of the flower was real and warm and also wet. And the wet was rising to my chin. Suddenly there was a noise. I opened my eyes. Francis, who was lying half against and half on top of me, licking my cheek, sneezed, and I realized that that was the second sneeze, and that the sound that had wakened me was the sound of the first. I put my hand to my cheek. It was hot, and I knew that I had fallen asleep in the sun. For a minute I lay there, remembering the marvelous happiness that had made me laugh, and feeling the laugh still bubbling inside me. Then, yawning, I tried to sit up. Francis, who was still on me, almost fell off.

"Ummm," I said, lying down again. I put my arm around him.

In a minute he took off and then came back with his stick, which he pushed against my nose.

"All right," I said, and sat up. About to throw the stick, I paused. Far off, at the bottom of the field, where the ground was lower and flatter, Tony and a friend of his were running. Being above, I could see them easily. Both had on running shorts and tank tops. They didn't even appear to be trying hard, but their long muscular legs seemed to eat up the ground. They looked wonderful. I sat there for a moment, Francis's stick in my hand. I wish I could run like that, I thought suddenly. Then I threw the stick.

"Guess what?" Dr. Brand said when I visited him on Monday. "You've lost five pounds."

The joy that went through me, making me feel as though I blushed all over, was quickly tempered by a rather spooky thought. Five pounds. Wasn't that exactly what I'd told Dottie I'd lost?

"That's funny," I said.

"What?" Dr. Brand asked. I didn't like him, because the moment I looked at him I felt as though I weighed five hundred pounds. But, aside from that, he wasn't too bad. He had black hair and a short, trim black beard.

"I told a friend of mine that I'd lost five pounds."

"So what's wrong with that? You have."

"But I hadn't weighed myself when I said that. Do you think I can tell the future?"

"It's more likely that your body knows how much you've lost and conveys that information to you."

"It sounds pretty weird."

"There are lots of weird things about the mind and the body and the relationship between the two. We haven't even begun to learn about that. Are you finding it hard to lose weight?"

Truthfully, I wasn't, most of the time. What with Francis and cleaning up after him and going to see Sister Elizabeth, I'd been too busy. On the other hand, there'd been that time when the chocolate bars, which I had still not removed from my laundry bag, had been floating around in my head like giant blimps with chocolate-peanut fins, trailing long streamers of delicious smells.

"Sort of," I said.

"That brings us down to one seventeen," Dr. Brand said, adjusting the scale and then pushing down his glasses so he could make sure he had the number right. "Only twenty-seven more to go. But it should be a breeze now. Once you've started it gets a lot easier."

Twenty-seven pounds, I thought. There was a girl in our class who said she weighed seventy-four pounds. She was small and frail-looking and tough as anything. She was on practically every sports team. When she jumped over the horse in gym she just seemed to fly, as though wires were attached to her shoulders. I now had to lose—I did some quick mental arithmetic—more than a third of her weight.

"You okay?" Dr. Brand said.

I got off the scale. "Yes."

"How did you like Sister Elizabeth?"

"I liked her," I said without enthusiasm. I wished all the people who were trying to get me thin would stop talking about her. It spoiled her for me.

"She's one of the best nutritionists in the state," Dr. Brand said.

"Then why's she a nun?"

"I don't know. I guess she was what they call a vocation. You'd better ask her that yourself."

I put on my jacket.

"I want you back here for another weigh-in in two weeks," Dr. Brand said.

"Okay."

He patted me on the shoulder. "With that red hair and those green eyes, you're a very pretty girl."

Warmth startled all over me. Then he spoiled it.

Dr. Brand smiled. "Or you will be—when you've lost that flab."

The warmth turned to anger. It was hard not to cry. "You mean I'll never have a boyfriend until I lose weight."

"I didn't say that. You did." He looked up from the file he was writing in and said, "Let's put it this way: Do you like fat boys?"

I thought of Horace Lang. He was terribly fat. And repulsive. The other boys made fun of him. Now he ran errands for them. His nickname was Gofer Lang. Then I thought of the even fatter boys I'd seen up at St. Monica's.

Dr. Brand was watching me. "You see now why it's so important to lose weight," he said.

I felt desperate. He didn't seem to care about anything concerning me except my weight. "I have a dog named Francis and I'm trying to housebreak him," I said.

"Really? Watch those calories now. No desserts. No candy. And try to do as much exercise as you can. See you in a couple of weeks."

I looked at him for a minute. I wanted to cry so much my throat ached. To him I wasn't even a person. I was just a body entirely surrounded by fat. Nothing else mattered. Ms. Fat. I watched him as he scribbled in his records. He wasn't even listening. I decided to try an experiment.

"I also have a large bull elephant," I said slowly. "Purple. The trouble is, he pees on Mother's carpet."

"That could be a problem," Dr. Brand said absently, still writing in his records. "How many calories a day did we put you on?"

"Twenty-five thousand, four hundred sixty-nine and a half," I said.

"Ummm. Well, be extra careful about staying within them now, won't you? And then maybe you'll have lost another five pounds by the time I see you next."

"Right," I said. "I'll stay within them."

"Did you read the book on living with a dog?" Sister Elizabeth asked the next afternoon.

"Part of it," I said. I had read about half the night before in bed before going to sleep. "I like it. She really likes dogs, doesn't she? You know, I was thinking, if she was a graduate from St. Monica's, she must have been disabled. What was the matter with her?"

"She had a form of cerebral palsy, as Sebastian does, so that it was difficult for her to walk properly. But she worked hard at her exercises, and by now it would be hard to tell without watching her for a while that she'd had any problem. But she had to work to get into a premedical course at college and then veterinarian training."

I thought about that for a while. "Did you work with her?"

"Oh yes. She was particularly interested in nutrition, because she wanted to get as much mileage, so to speak, out of healthy eating as she could. And I knew how she felt, because as a child I had polio and took up nutrition—along with endless exercises—to build up my leg muscles."

"I thought nobody got polio these days."

"Not often. But sometimes." She paused. "Did you read the book on foods and nutrients?"

I shook my head. "No." I had thrown it on my desk and was now a little sorry I hadn't even looked at it. My mind slid back to the woman who had written the book on dogs. "You mean she—the vet who wrote the book—studied food to help her overcome being disabled?"

"Yes. Did you know that you can take a perfectly healthy infant and, by denying it the right food, not only impede its growth, but damage its brain? You must have seen pictures of badly nourished or starving children. Unfortunately, there are far too many of them around the world. But the opposite holds true also: healthy eating is essential to make the best of whatever you have."

I nodded and looked down at Francis, who had collapsed on the newspaper-covered floor and gone to sleep. Sister Elizabeth had put down newspapers especially for him, as she had the previous time, which was nice of her. It was funny, I reflected. Whenever I thought of food I thought of ice cream and cookies, which the whole world was busy telling me all the time I couldn't have, or I thought about things like spinach and brussels sprouts and broccoli, which I hated, partly because they were hateable, but mostly because they were what everybody thought I should be eating instead of what I wanted. And then here was this woman who had thought about food as something to make her physically better so she could be a vet.

"I guess I'll read the book on food tonight," I said. And then I burst out, "I must say I think it was unfair of God to put all the calories in ice cream and all the vitamins in spinach."

Sister Elizabeth laughed. "You know, Dinah, if you

could think of eating healthily as something you're doing for yourself, instead of as a deprivation other people are forcing on you, I think you'd find it a lot easier." She put her head on one side. "Do you know what I'm talking about?"

"I suppose so."

"In an odd way you make me think of my brother—" She stopped.

"Was he fat?"

"No. Not fat. But all his life, even as a child, he did everything with great intensity. One of his teachers once said that he was the kind of person who believed that if one pill was good for you, then the whole box would be even better. Years later, he told me he'd always felt he had this empty place inside him he called The Hole, and he said he'd spent his entire life trying to fill it, and with all the wrong things. In his teens he got into pills and drugs and liquor, and by the time he was thirty, he'd been in I don't know how many hospitals and rehabilitation places and was told that if he took one more drink or another pill he'd either kill himself or land in a mental institution." She glanced at me. "I don't mean to compare the two of you in that way, only in what he said about himself. He told me that as he lay there in the hospital that final time he knew he could never in the world just stay away from all that—he'd have to put something in its place."

I remembered the monster-shaped space inside me from my dream. "So what did he put in its place?"

"Oh—a whole different philosophy. Instead of thinking of himself as a body perpetually hungry for something he never found, he came to think of his body as a dwelling place that he had been given and that he had to care for in order to live his life here on earth as well and fully as possible. The way you care for Francis, for example." She looked down at him. "You wouldn't give him food you knew was bad for him, would you? Not if you wanted him to enjoy his life and his body, so he could run around and be free and healthy."

I was staring at Francis. "I have Francis," I said. "Maybe, if I tried, I could put caring about him in the place of eating."

"Francis is wonderful, but he isn't a substitute for doing something for yourself—for your own body."

"Didn't Sebastian and the vet you were talking about do that with animals?"

"No. Sebastian loves his animals. Helen MacNair, the vet, does, too. But they don't—and didn't—use them as substitutes for something else."

I thought about this. "You mean caring for Francis instead of eating would be using him?"

"You wouldn't be doing it deliberately, Dinah. Of course not. But to expect Francis to make up for all the people who humiliate you, and for feeling deprived when you can't eat sweets, is too much of a burden for one small dog—or even a large one. Sooner or later he wouldn't be enough. He'd fail, and then I'm afraid you'd resent him."

"Resent *Francis?* I wouldn't!"

"All right, Dinah, I believe you. But as things are, I think you feel as angry as you do because you're facing an unacceptable choice: on one side is eating what you want but being constantly criticized and humiliated for being fat; on the other side is going on a diet and losing weight, which will stop you feeling put down, but will make you feel deprived. That's an ugly situation to be in—like being caught between the jaws of a crocodile. Now you're saying that caring for Francis can take you out of that dilemma, that because of him you won't feel either humiliated or deprived. And that's what bothers me. What happens when you discover it doesn't work? How will you feel about Francis then? I don't think that anything outside yourself, including Francis, can get you off this particular hot seat. The only way you won't feel deprived when you adhere to a food program—or any other regimen that consists of your not doing something you want very much to do—is to do it solely for yourself, and because, on a deep level, you're willing to give up one thing to gain another. *Not* to please other people, or to buy their goodwill. To expect poor Francis to compensate for all the self-denial involved in going on a diet is about as useful as doing it to please your mother, which won't work either."

Sister Elizabeth paused and then said, "Think, Dinah—is there anything you want very much for yourself?"

I was about to say no, vigorously, when suddenly, as though I could see him, I had a clear picture of my brother Tony—running.

"Tony, my brother, runs," I said.

"So did my brother, the one I was telling you about. That was the first thing he started putting in the place of all the things he'd stopped putting inside himself. It took him a long while, of course, to build up strength. But he's become a fine runner for his age. He ran the Boston Marathon three times and is planning to run again next year."

"Tony wants to do that. How long is it?"

"Twenty-six miles, three hundred and eight-five yards." Sister Elizabeth smiled. "I ran it once."

"Did you? Before you were a nun?"

"That's right. I went at it slowly, ran a bit and walked a bit, then ran some more. I built up gradually and easily, without pushing myself. Eventually, I tried a mini-marathon of about six miles." She paused and looked at me. "You could do the same, you know. Start slow. Try a mile or a mile and a half of running and walking and see how you like it. You might not like it at all, in which case you could try something else. But then again you might like it. Why don't you think about it?"

"Me?" I glanced down and saw the curve of my belly sticking out so far I couldn't see my toes. All of a sudden I could feel my body's weight and fatness. A terrible hatred of it filled me and I saw, in my mind, the kids' faces in gym when I tried to jump over the horse. They'd die laughing if anyone told them I was trying to run. My hatred turned into anger. I looked up at the tall, slender nun. "You're making fun of me," I almost shouted.

"I am *not*. I would never, never do such a thing. Why should I?" She hesitated, and I had the odd feeling that she was seeing all the pictures that were in my mind. "Nobody has to know. You don't have to do it in front of people. Get up early, when the sun comes up. It's beautiful then. Take Francis out. You have a ready-made excuse there. Walk a bit and run a bit. But walk three times as much as you run at first. And never push yourself. It'll come. Call Dr. Brand and check with him. But I'm pretty sure he'll approve. According to the note he sent me, you're very healthy."

"Except for my weight." My heart gave a thump. "You mean running will help me to lose?"

"Not directly, and certainly not right away. You'd have to run a mile to run off the calories in a piece of bread or an apple. But one of the things I discovered when I ran was that—on the whole, and over a long period—I was less hungry, and I ate less."

"Truly?"

"Truly. And eventually, if you keep at it for several months, it *will* help with your weight. And one other thing—don't tell anyone, I mean except Dr. Brand. Not because it's wrong, or for the reason you were thinking—that people would laugh. But if you keep it a secret, at first, anyway, it will be yours, something for yourself that you can think about when people are trying to make you be something you don't want to be, or trying to pressure you in some way."

"I thought everybody was supposed to share everything."

"Not everything, and not all the time. Later, when—and if—you become a steady runner and really know you can do it, then you can share it. But right now, except for Dr. Brand and Francis—" she smiled down at him—"don't tell anybody."

"You know," I said suddenly, "I've lost five pounds since Dr. Brand weighed me two weeks ago. When I got on the scale yesterday, in his office, I was five pounds lighter."

"That's wonderful, Dinah! I'm surprised you didn't tell me that right away."

The moment she said that I realized I was surprised, too. "I guess I felt it almost didn't count because I wasn't trying to lose. It just happened because I was so busy with Francis I didn't get around to eating a lot of the junk I usually do."

"So because you didn't actually suffer, you feel you

can't take pleasure in it? You must be one of the last of the Puritans, Dinah!"

"Somebody else said that—the actress who gave me Francis." And I explained about the dollar.

"Well, try to feel good about it. Because some of the pounds come off painlessly shouldn't make losing them any less satisfying. And remember, you lost weight not just because you didn't eat candy and ice cream, but because you ate fewer calories. No matter how many weird diets people think up, that's all still the name of the game, calories; you put in so many, you burn up so many.

"The reason sweets are considered bad is that they're high in calories and low in food value—there's no real nourishment in them. But you lost over the last two weeks because you took in fewer calories. In other words, feeling deprived is not what makes you lose weight. Dinah, this may sound like a distinction without a difference, but it's terribly important, because I think it's the nub of your problem. It's eating fewer calories that will make you lose weight, *not* the feeling of deprivation. An eight- or nine-ounce steak is as high in calories as a hot fudge sundae, although a steak will give your body better nourishment than a sundae. But a thousand calories is a thousand calories. Do you understand what I'm saying?"

"Yes," I said. "I guess so."

"So, your losing five pounds, even though you weren't trying, is great. Feel happy about it. All of those terrible clichés about the beginning of the longest journey is a step and one day at a time and the best way to get something done is to begin are true. They helped me a lot when I was trying to learn how to walk. I didn't care whether they were corny or not. I'd mutter to myself things like, 'Yard by yard it's hard, but inch by inch it's a cinch,' as I did all those slow, boring, painful exercises." She smiled, and I saw her eyelids tilt up at the corners. "Now, I was wondering if you and Francis would like to go and give Sebastian a hand. The rabbits got loose and caused general havoc in the zoo, and he's trying to clean up."

"Sure."

Sister Elizabeth took us as far as the door. "Do you know the way? Straight ahead—you can't miss it."

I nodded.

"What bus are you going to take?"

"The five o'clock, I guess."

"I'll come for you then."

Sebastian was poking lettuce through the square-holed wiring in front of the rabbit compound. Francis and I went over and stood beside him and watched. After feeding two of the rabbits, he pushed his hand through the big wire squares and stroked them between their ears and along their backs. But he was careful with the third, a big gray one with huge ears, and kept several inches of lettuce between him and the rabbit's teeth.

"Does he bite?" I said.

"Sometimes. He doesn't mean to. He just gets nervous, especially if someone else is here."

"Maybe you'd rather I left," I said huffily.

"No. I like you to be here." He spoke each word carefully, and I remembered about his speech impediment.

"Really?"

"Yes." His head jerked a little. "I asked S-S-S Sister Elizabeth when you'd be here."

It would have been really super if those words had

come from Tony's friend, the one with blond hair and high cheekbones. But they hadn't. They'd come from Sebastian. And then I hated myself for wondering if he thought he could say it to me because I was a freak, too.

". . . and so he's always been cranky," Sebastian finished. When I didn't say anything, he turned from the big rabbit he'd been talking about and looked at me with a funny, worried expression on his face. "Did I say something wrong?"

"No. Hey—watch out! Your finger!"

Sebastian snatched his finger back just in time. I was glad his attention was distracted. But it wasn't distracted for long. He gave the rabbit the rest of the lettuce and said again, "Did I s-say something to make you feel funny or mad?"

"No." And then I said, "I'm glad to be here, too." I wanted to get off the subject, so I went on quickly, "Sister Elizabeth said your rabbits got out and messed everything up. It looks okay to me."

"I still have to put those boxes straight. And they ate a whole bunch of radishes."

"I'll help," I said. Francis had flopped down where he was and gone to sleep.

Sebastian showed me how to pile the boxes. I noticed that, as he put one after the other out by the garbage, he would check something off in a book. He did everything slowly, and his writing hand and one leg sometimes shook.

"Would you like me to help you with that?" I said. The moment I said it I knew it was the wrong thing to say.

"No thanks. It would t-t-take longer to exp-p-plain than it takes t-t-to do. Besides, I d-d-don't need help."

After a minute I said, "I'm sorry. I didn't mean . . ." I was about to say "that you needed help." That's exactly what I had meant. But ". . . to say anything wrong," I finally finished.

He closed the book and then got another, smaller box of some kind of feed and went to the gerbils' cage.

"It's ok-k-kay," he said. "Some p-p-people think because I c-c-can't talk and walk properly—" he took a deep breath—"I c-c-can't do anything." This time his stammer was marked.

Once, at a school I'd been to, there'd been a sort of in-group of girls that I'd tried to join. I kept running up when they were together. Finally one of them, a pretty, dark girl who seemed to be a leader, looked at me and said, "Why don't you run away? You're N period O period O period U period." The others giggled.

"What's that?" I asked.

"You'll find out," she said coolly. "Come on, you guys."

I finally asked another girl. "What does N period O period O period U period mean?" I said it as casually as I could, as though it didn't matter.

She looked at me and grinned. "Why? Did somebody say it to you?"

I shrugged.

She grinned more broadly. "It means Not One Of Us."

Hearing what Sebastian had just said, the whole thing came back to me like a TV movie. That's what they would have said to Sebastian, too. And that's what they would have said at the school I went to now, if they'd known it, to Sebastian—and also to me.

I thought about the girl who'd been here and was now a vet. They'd have said it to her, too.

"Do you know the vet who used to be a student here and wrote a book about living with a dog?" I asked.

"Dr. Helen MacNair? Sure. I write to her all the time, and she writes me back."

After that we were both quiet while Sebastian fed the gerbils and I watched. Then Sister Elizabeth appeared in the door.

"Bus time, Dinah," she said.

"Good-bye," I said to Sebastian. "Come on, Francis." I picked up the end of the leash.

"'Bye." Sebastian leaned down and patted Francis as he passed by.

"Here," Sister Elizabeth said, opening a door that led outside. "It's such a nice day, we might as well walk outside rather than through the school building."

Francis and I followed her down the steps. "Doesn't Sebastian have to take a bus?"

"Yes. He usually catches the five-thirty. Or sometimes one of our counselors who drives down drops him off."

"I guess that's easier for him."

"It is, of course. But Sebastian is very dogged about doing things the way everybody else does. He hates having special favors. And we support him in that whenever we can."

I remembered what he'd said to me about not needing any help. "He doesn't like people to help him. He said so."

"He likes to get that straight with everybody right away. He's very bright, and he pretty much knows that what he does with the rest of his life depends on him. That's why he takes the hard line he does, and I respect him for it."

"Did he ever go to a regular school, like the one down in the village that I go to?"

"Yes. For a while." We paused while Francis started making a close investigation of some tree roots. "He had a rather bad time there. Not because everyone was unkind to him. Many weren't, and some were really nice. But the few who weren't nice, weren't nice at all. I think he could have stood that, but his awareness of it and the tension it caused exaggerated his symptoms. He stammered far more and had far less control over his limbs than he does now. By the time he got an answer out in class almost no one, including a lot of teachers, could see that he was bright and quick. Then his mother sent him here, and he's streaked ahead in every area. But I think his memory of that time at the public school hardened his resolve not to make any concessions to his illness, and not let anyone else do so, either."

"Do all the kids here have some problem?"

"Yes, of one kind of another. Some are partly paralyzed, some have hearing problems and some have only partial sight. Some have difficulty walking, and some are retarded."

It sounded, somehow, depressing. "Do you like working with kids like that? Or are you doing it as a good deed or something?"

"I don't think so-called good deeds are any good if you hate doing them. Everybody has to get something out of it, including the person who's doing it. I think Francis has finished his personal toilet. We can go across here."

"But what do you get out of it?" I said after a min-

ute. It sounded awful, but there was no way of saying
it to make it sound better.

She didn't answer for a minute. "I guess the best
way I can describe it is that I feel the way a gardener
does when he plants something, then waters it and
sees it come up."

I waited for her to say something else, but she
didn't.

Suddenly I found myself wanting a hot fudge sundae so much I could see and smell it. Especially smell
it. It was terribly real. In fact, so real . . . "I smell
something terribly good, like a chocolate sundae," I
said. "Like chocolate, anyway. Can you smell it?"

Sister Elizabeth looked down at me and smiled. "It
does smell delicious, doesn't it? We're passing the
kitchen, and I guess they must be making some kind
of dessert, because what we're smelling is vanilla."

Maybe it was because the smell was so real and
powerful that I found myself thinking that if I did
break my promise to Mother, I could smuggle Francis
up here, instead of taking him to the humane society,
and I could come and see him. And then, perhaps because I was thinking that and it seemed such an obvious solution, I had the strangest feeling. It was as
though I was standing at the end of a long, long corridor. The corridor was my life, and for all the rest of it
I could have sundaes and candy or Francis, but never
both.

"The bus will be by here in about seven minutes,"
Sister Elizabeth said. "I'll walk across to the gate with
you."

"All right."

We walked in silence for a while. And then she said,
"What's the matter?"

"Nothing," I said.

"You know I don't think that's true, Dinah. It's not nothing. You are a person of powerful feelings, and I can feel them. You don't have to tell me if you don't want to. But I don't think we ought to pretend."

So I told her about the corridor.

"You know, if you thought you had to do anything for the rest of your life every single day—like brushing your teeth—it would look like an awful burden. Try not thinking about anything but tomorrow. It's much easier that way. Truly." We walked on for a bit and then she said, "Have you had a problem with your weight for a long time, or just recently?"

"According to pictures, I looked pretty ordinary till I was about five. After that, well, I started getting fat."

"Did anything different happen in your life then?"

"I don't know exactly. I stayed with my grandmother, Mother's mother, for a year when Mother and Daddy were in India. Granny was like Mrs. Lewis—she always said she liked fat little girls. Somehow, when somebody says that now, I want to stop eating—for about a minute. Anyway, when I wasn't with Granny, I would go and be with Mother and Daddy for a while. Only when we were abroad they had to go out a lot at night, and I'd be left with a sitter or a maid or something. I used to be scared that they'd be killed on the way home. And I'd get out of my bed and pray and pray and pray. Then, when I got back in, I'd be afraid that I hadn't said the prayers the right way or had forgotten to say 'amen' or something, so I'd have to get out of bed again and do them all over. And then I'd get back in again and start to worry that I'd said them wrong. It was awful."

"It sounds worse than awful. Why were you so afraid they'd be killed?"

"I don't know. I can't remember."

"How long did it go on for?"

"I can't remember that either. I just remember doing it a lot, and then, later, not at all. Maybe a year."

"And did you eat then, when you were afraid, or before?"

"Yes. When we were abroad and had a maid I used to tell her to bring me sandwiches. She didn't like it, and Mother got very angry with me when she found out. So I'd buy candy of some kind and hide it."

By this time we'd reached the gate. The bus came around the corner and stopped and, with a wheeze, opened its door. "Congratulations," Sister Elizabeth said, "on the five pounds." She smiled and I grinned back at her. Then Francis and I got on the bus.

"See you day after tomorrow," I yelled at her. As the bus pulled out, I watched her standing there like a tall black needle. Just as we were about to go around the corner, Sister Elizabeth waved.

SIX

I really felt good on the way home. Suddenly the five pounds I'd lost seemed terribly important. I hadn't allowed myself to think about it last night, but talking to Sister Elizabeth had made a difference. It was okay to care. I stared at my image in the bus window and tried to see if I looked as though I'd lost weight. It seemed to me, being as objective as I could, that I did look a little thinner. And as soon as I thought that, I felt thinner.

"I've lost five pounds," I said, very quietly, to Francis.

He was sprawled on the seat beside me, his head on my leg, his eyes closed. But at that he opened his eyes and wagged his backside a little.

"Thank you," I said, taking it as a compliment.

For the rest of the bus ride I tried to make up my mind whether I would tell Mother about the five pounds immediately, and get her instant approval, or wait until I lost the next five, so I could say casually,

"By the way, according to Dr. Brand's scale, I've lost *ten* pounds," which was really a lot. Or even say nothing at all, but wait for her to notice; the fantasy was as vivid as a movie. "Dinah, darling, you look *thin*, you must have lost *pounds*. James, Brenda, Tony, Jack, just look at Dinah, how *thin* she is. Darling, your clothes hang on you. . . ." Without thinking, I put my hand to my shirt to see how much I could gather up in front. Not a great deal, but perhaps, I thought, more than last week. Yes, I was sure it was more than last week. I seemed to remember having trouble buttoning some of the buttons. "See, Francis, how loose it is?" Francis snored.

"Hey, you!"

I jumped. The bus driver was peering around the back of his seat, and the other passengers were gazing at me.

"Isn't this your stop?" the bus driver said.

I looked around. We were at the bottom of the hill below the street where I lived.

"Yes!" I leapt up. I snatched Francis and I hurried out of the bus. "Sorry," I muttered, as I got off.

"Boy, you were far away," the bus driver said. "I hope it was a nice dream." Then he grinned, closed the door and drove off.

I felt a little foolish, but went back immediately to trying to decide whether I was going to tell Mother now or later about losing weight. I still hadn't come to any conclusion when I arrived at our house—or at least I didn't think I had. But I must have, because the moment I walked into the kitchen and saw Mother I started, "Mom, guess what! I lost—"

Mother had had her back to me, stirring something in a pan, but as soon as I said the first words she turned around. "Dinah," she said, interrupting me, "something's come up that I want to talk to you about." She put the spoon on the kitchen table and came over.

"Okay, Mom. But listen, guess what—"

"Later, Dinah, this is really important." She took a breath. "I want you to be particularly nice to Brenda this evening." She stopped.

It was funny, I thought, staring at her. When she said those words everything I had in my head, all the words I was going to say, just stopped. They didn't vanish. I could remember them, but it was as though they had come to a high wall and there was no way I could get them over.

"Dinah, are you listening to me?" Mother's voice was kind, and she had put her hand against my cheek, the way I had imagined she would when I told her that I had lost five pounds, or she discovered that I had. "Why, lambie," she would say, her hand on my cheek, "how absolutely marvelous. . . . You really mustn't overdo it, though."

"Dinah, are you listening to me?" For a minute the words didn't mean anything. And then suddenly they did.

"Brenda," I said, and I could feel the anger, like heat, starting inside me.

"Yes. Brenda. Please, Dinah, you must listen. It's very important that we're all particularly nice to her this evening and make her feel that she is part of the family."

"Why?" I asked. In a detached way I was curious about what Mother was going to say. But much louder and closer was a voice in my head that was insisting that Mother simply hadn't heard what I had said to her, which was why she hadn't responded and was talking instead about Brenda. "Mother—" I said loudly.

"Yes, darling. In a minute. Just let me explain about this, because I think sometimes you haven't really understood about Brenda."

I didn't say anything.

Mother had taken her hand away. "Now listen, lambie, Brenda got a letter today from her father saying he wouldn't be coming back home for his summer leave the way he planned. You know he was supposed to come here first, then he and Brenda were going to go off on a trip together. And after that he was going to try to be assigned to the States. But something has come up about his job, and he can't make it this year at all. Brenda is terribly upset. You can see why. So I want you to go out of your way to be friendly to her. Okay?"

I pushed my anger down. I would be nice to Brenda, then maybe everyone would be pleased when I told them about the five pounds I had lost.

"Okay," I said.

"And go up and put on a dress for dinner. That shirt is dirty, and, anyway, I'm trying to make it a special occasion."

"I'll put on another shirt," I said. I didn't like dresses much.

Mother had turned back to her casserole. "All right. If you'd rather. Mrs. Lewis put clean shirts in your drawer this afternoon, didn't you, Mrs. Lewis?" She glanced up at the housekeeper.

"That's right. And I hung up your clean jeans in your closet."

"Fine," Mother said. "You could put them on, too, if

you want, Dinah. Those jeans you have on are so filthy we could get a summons from the Department of Health. They practically stand up by themselves. Put them in the laundry. Run along, darling, and get into your clean clothes. Dinner will be on soon."

It was when I was going through the hall to the stairs that I had my brain wave. It was true that I hated to wear dresses, mostly because I felt fatter in them than in jeans and a shirt hanging outside. But there was a dress that Mother had bought me last year, a green and white dress with a zip up the back that I hadn't worn this spring for the simple reason that it wouldn't quite close. Maybe now, with the five pounds off, I would be able to zip it up. Mother would see immediately that I had lost the five pounds, and so would the others.

I turned the corner of the stairs and started up. From the bottom step I could see into the living room. Brenda and Daddy were in there staring at the evening news on television. All I could see of Brenda's face was her profile, so I couldn't really tell whether she was upset or not. But she certainly seemed to be calm enough, so I decided that Mother was exaggerating. At least, I thought, heading for the bedroom, with Francis following on my heels, I'd have the bedroom to myself for a while.

"Come on in, Francis," I said, and shut the door as soon as he scuttled in.

For once I regretted my untidy habits. When I finally pulled the green and white dress out of the jumble of clothes packed into my half of the closet, it badly needed ironing.

"If I had this closet to myself," I said angrily to Francis, who was scuffling around the closet floor

among the shoes, "my clothes wouldn't be so crowded
and they wouldn't get so wrinkled." I glanced across
the wooden center partition towards Brenda's half.
Was it because the hangers in my half were jammed
together every which way that my clothes were so
wrinkled, or was it because Brenda had fewer clothes?
I did a hasty count. Brenda had fewer clothes. They
were also mounted evenly on their hangers, collars and
seams straight, all the same distance from one another. Well, I thought, I can use the iron and ironing
board in the hall linen closet.

Ironing the dress must have taken longer than I realized, because I had barely turned off the iron, taken
off my shirt and jeans, and put on some sandals when
I heard Mother's voice. "Dinah, dinner's ready! Come
on down."

"Coming!" I yelled, and slipped the dress over my
head.

After a few minutes of tugging at the zipper, first
from the bottom and then from the top, I finally got it
closed. Sucking in my stomach and holding my
breath, I turned sideways and looked at myself in the
mirror. I definitely looked thinner, I decided, and relaxed a little. But the moment I relaxed wrinkles appeared at my waist and under my breasts, so that
there were three bulges, one on top of another. First
there was my chest, then a crease, then my dia-
phragm, then another crease, and at the bottom another and much bigger bulge, which was my stomach.
Well, I'd just have to remember to hold everything in,
and anyway, the zipper closed, which *proved* I was
thinner.

"I'll put you in the kitchen," I said to Francis. I ran
downstairs with him at my heels, hastily spread news-

paper on the floor of one corner of the kitchen, and kissed him between the ears. "When you're a little older and better trained, you can stay in the living room with Brewster, but right now I'd better leave you here." Then I said to him again, sort of rehearsing, "I lost five pounds. *Five* pounds," I repeated.

Francis was a truly great dog. He wagged his tail. I went into the dining room.

"Hi," I said as I walked in. I really felt terrific.

Mother was busy talking to Brenda, who was sitting beside her and didn't look up. I could see then that Brenda's eyes were red, and the end of her nose looked pink.

"Come in, come in," Daddy said, pushing out the chair next to him. He was talking in what I always think of as his phony-jovial voice, which usually means that he is trying to pretend that there hasn't been a fight or some other kind of upset and that everything is fine.

"*Asseyez-vous,*" Daddy said, patting the chair.

"What's that?" Jack asked.

"It's French for sit down," I told him, glad that I knew it.

"That is, if you can," Tony said, grinning, his eye on my middle.

Daddy glanced at me and away. There was a funny look on his face. "Okay, Tony, knock it off," he said.

Mother looked up. "What's Tony been up to?" she asked, and then turned back and smiled at Brenda. I remembered what she had said about making Brenda feel like a member of the family. The whole thing reminded me of something my brother Donald once said. I think it was at a Thanksgiving when we were all together. "Mom's being very groupy," he'd commented. And when I'd asked him what he meant, he'd said, "Oh, she puts on an 'aren't-we-all-having-fun-together' act." At the time, I hadn't really been sure what he meant, but now I knew. She was doing it for Brenda, to make her feel so much a part of the family that she wouldn't mind her father's not coming home.

I sat down and glanced across at Brenda. In the pink evening light from the window I could see the shine of wet right below one eye. I knew she was miserable, but I couldn't feel sorry for her. I tried to think about how I would feel if my father weren't coming home for a year, but all I could think about was the fact that nobody was noticing that I had lost five pounds. And then, before I knew I was going to say anything, and before I remembered that I was going to be nice to Brenda first, the words popped out of my mouth.

"I've lost five pounds," I said.

"Maybe you should have waited until you lost another five—or ten," Tony said, grinning again. "You're putting a powerful strain on those seams."

"Well, last fall I couldn't even get into it, and now I can."

"With a shoehorn?"

"You think you're so funny," Jack said to Tony. "You crack me up."

"Okay, now, kids." Daddy was still being jovial. "Let's not have the five hundred and fourteenth skirmish in the Randall Peloponnesian Wars. Dinah, honey, it may be a tight squeeze, but it looks fine."

"It'll look even better ten pounds from now, if Dinah gets there," Tony said.

"Why don't you shut up?" I yelled at him. All of a sudden I didn't feel thin anymore.

"What on earth are you shouting about?" Mother asked. She and Brenda had been talking, but both were now looking at me. And I saw something that made me even madder. For a second, or maybe even less, Brenda's eyes widened, and there was an odd, satisfied look on her face. Then she looked down.

"'And the lion and the lamb shall lie down together,'" Daddy said in a mock-serious voice, still trying to get general harmony started. "Now let's all enjoy the peaceable kingdom. Brenda, would you like a roll?"

"No thank you," Brenda said in a small voice. "I'm not hungry."

"Dinah?" Daddy was holding the plate in front of me.

I hesitated for a second. I was suddenly ravenously hungry, but a whole lot of things—my diet, hunger, Sister Elizabeth, running, my green and white dress and the fact that I could hardly breathe in it—all seemed to knock against one another in my head. Hunger won. I reached out my hand just as Daddy, thinking, I guess, that I wasn't going to take a roll, swung the plate over towards Jack. Instead of my fingers closing over the roll, I knocked it off the plate and then tried to catch it, hitting the gravy dish. I saw the whole thing in slow motion—the gravy dish toppling over, a brown stream flowing across the white tablecloth.

"Oh, Dinah!" Mother wailed. "That's your grandmother's damask cloth, the last one we have. I put it on specially for Brenda."

By this time Mother was on her feet. Jack had pushed away from the table because the gravy was beginning to drip over the side, and Daddy was trying to mop it up with his napkin.

"Not with your napkin," Mother cried. "I'll get a cloth."

She shoved back her chair and left the room. In about two seconds she had returned with a dish towel in her hand. "The least you could do, Dinah, since you started the disaster, is to help. Go to the kitchen and bring back some paper towels."

"I'll go, Aunt Lorna," Brenda said.

"Thank you, Brenda," Mother said. "I'm sorry our dinner has turned out such a mess. Dinah, don't just stand there!"

I went into the kitchen and took a towel off the rack above the sink. Brenda was busy pulling sheets off the roll of paper towels. Without looking at me, she trotted back to the dining room.

Mother was mopping up the gravy with the green paper toweling Brenda had brought when I arrived with the dish towel. "Here," I said, and held it out to her.

"I don't need it. I used the paper towels. You can take this back to the kitchen, though." And she handed me a slimy brown ball of gravy-soaked green paper. "Be careful how you carry it. This is the first time you've worn that dress since it was cleaned."

"I lost five pounds," I said. "That's why I could put it on."

Mother glanced at me. As her gaze flickered over my stomach, I could feel my bulges go out like so many balloons. "Tony was right," Mother said. "You should lose five or ten more before you try to wear that dress. It's far too tight."

"You see?" Tony said. He was sitting tilted back in

his chair and grinning at me. Something went off BOOM inside me. Gripping the brown greasy ball of paper towels, I went over to him and pushed it in his face and rubbed it all over his hair before he knew what I was doing.

"You sadist!" I yelled at him. "I wish you were dead. I wish you'd die horribly!"

He was pushing at the paper towels and trying to stand up. Tony is athletic and a lot stronger than I am, but the paper towels were slick and he couldn't get a grip on them or on my hand. Before he managed to stand up, I'd not only smeared his face and hair, I'd gotten a lot of gravy on his shirt and trousers.

"Get off me!" he shouted, pushing the paper towels away and springing up.

"Stop that at once, Dinah!" Mother said. "What on earth has got into you? You must be crazy. Here I asked you particularly to help us make it a nice evening, and first you put on a dress that makes every pound stick out, then you knock over the gravy dish, and then you attack Tony simply because he points out the obvious."

Whatever it was that had gone BOOM in my head exploded again. I turned and threw the gravy-soaked ball of paper across the room. It went within an inch of Mother's head and hit the wall behind, making a big splat.

"Dinah!" Daddy said. "Until now I've been on your side. But I will not put up with physical violence. Apologize to your mother and Tony."

"I will not," I said. "You're a rotten family. You always talk about family togetherness, but nobody's on my side. You bug me and bug me and bug me to lose weight, like it was the most important thing in the

world, and then when I try to tell you that I've lost
five pounds, you won't even listen. All you think
about is that I'm fat. Nothing else matters. I could
find the cure for cancer and it wouldn't matter, because I'm fat—"

"Dinah, will you stop yelling!" Mother said. "I told
you that Brenda—"

"And I'm sick of you always sticking up for Brenda!
I'm sorry she's not your daughter and I am, because
you like her a lot better. You shove her in my room
without even asking me, and you praise whatever she
does, and you ride me about eating, and you wouldn't
even have let me have Francis if Daddy hadn't said
to. And when I ask for a room of my own in the attic
you don't do anything about it. You don't even like
me. You hate me—"

"How can you say that, Dinah? It's wicked and it's
simply not true! Now stop—"

"I won't stop. I try and try and try, and I go up to see
Sister Elizabeth, and I think I can really do something
about putting something else in the place of eating, and
I put on this dress and all Tony does is make nasty
comments—"

"Okay, I'm sorry. I was just kidding. How was I to
know you're that sensitive?"

"Because you should have. We all should have
known."

Vaguely I heard Daddy's voice, but it was far away.
I felt as though words and feelings I had been dam-
ming up for a whole year were pouring out.

"I don't even feel like your daughter sometimes. I
wish I was an orphan. Then I could leave. I *wish* I
could leave. I wish I could never see you again, any of
you—"

"What have *I* done?" Jack said.

"You're thin and perfect, that's what you've done."

"Well, it's not my fault—"

"I suppose it's my fault that I'm so awful that like Daddy says, no boy will ever like me, and Tony's ashamed of me and Mother can't even think about anything except that I'm fat and Brenda's perfect. And I don't blame Brenda's father for staying away this year. If I was her father I'd stay away forever."

"Dinah!"

"I think she's a creep. I hate her. I don't want her in the room with me, and I wish I was dead. I wish I didn't have a body at all for everybody to hate, for no boy to like the way Daddy says, because—"

"Now just a minute—" Daddy put in.

"Yes, you did say that." Mother was shouting now. "That's nothing to what you've been doing to the poor child for the past year—"

"I suppose it's my fault, not—"

"And I hate it when you quarrel and yell at each other," I said. "I hate everybody," I said. "I hate myself because the only thing that matters is being thin. So I might as well be dead—"

Tears had been coming down my cheeks and I had been half crying, half shouting, but I really started to cry now, and when I saw Mother and Daddy coming towards me I knew I couldn't stand having them near me. I had to get away. So I ran to the back of the house, snatching my jacket off the hook in the hall as I went. I was running through people's backyards, on my way to the street leading into the fields, when I became aware of scampering feet behind me and heard a short bark. His tongue lolling out and his eyes bulging with pleasure, Francis flung himself at me.

"You'd better go home," I said, not really meaning it. And Francis knew I didn't mean it. He leapt around and then hurled himself forward, delighted that we were going to have this unexpected walk in the fields. Luckily, his leash was coiled up in one of my jacket's many pockets, so I snapped it on his collar until we got to the fields and I could let him loose. As we turned into the field, I noticed that while the sky on one side was still light, on the other it was not only getting dark, but there were big clouds, like dark gray cauliflower heads—it looked as though it was going to rain. I felt in one of my other pockets. Yes, the flashlight was there. Francis tugged at the leash and I let him loose.

I don't know how long Francis and I walked—or, at least, I walked and he darted and pounced through the undergrowth. Everything that had happened, everything I'd said and others had said, kept going through my mind: Mother's thinking about nothing but Brenda; Tony's smart-aleck remarks about my dress; Brenda's sitting there, Little Ms. Perfect, Little Ms. Thin; Mother's not even listening when I tried to tell her that I'd lost five pounds. . . . I went over and over the whole dinner scene, and each time I got angrier than ever and cried harder than before. Francis and I crossed and recrossed and went around the field, reaching the woods at the far side and then turning up to the edge of the woods that contained my tree and going around again. I knew the tree was where we'd end up, in the warm safe world of the Green Fat Kingdom or the Night Fat Kingdom, Francis in my jacket and both of us where no one would ever find us again. Because another dreary truth had become obvious to me in the long dark walk: Mother not only preferred Brenda to me, she would never like Francis, and, no matter what she'd promised, she would probably use the first excuse to send him off to the pound. But the tree and the Green Fat Kingdom would have to wait. For the moment I was filled with a strange, angry energy, and I had to keep moving.

Later—I don't know how much later—I finally slowed and came to a stop, aware of several facts. It was raining in a soft, damp drizzle, and had been for some time. The energy had steamed out of me, and most of my anger with it. Now I just felt drained and miserable. Not only was it raining, it was dark, although I could still make out the black of the trees and hill against the deep gray of the sky. In addition to all that, my feet were sore in several places, because walking through the fields in sandals was not the same as wearing sneakers. Standing there, with the wet sliding down my hair, I tried gingerly to wiggle my feet, and winced. Along with everything else, I had blisters.

Now, dimly, from far away, I heard Mother's cowbell ringing, and realized that it had sounded before but I had been too preoccupied to notice it. Mother was looking for me, and I knew I ought to go back. But I also knew that I couldn't.

"Francis?" I said.

A small wet ball of fur stepped onto my feet and stood there shivering. Various things I had read in the dog care book went through my mind. I should take him home and dry him off, I thought. And, again, knew I couldn't. I picked him up, put him down the front of my jacket and tied the belt, hoping that the jacket and my dress would dry him off. Then, with one arm around Francis, I set off in the direction of the tree.

Whether it was because my anger had burned itself out, or because I was tired, I didn't know. But when I started to go over all my grievances again—past, present, and probably future—my mind wandered off into a new fantasy.

"You're fat, you're fat, you're fat, you're fat, and nothing else matters," the World said, speaking in a voice that was strangely like Mother's. "It doesn't matter if you write plays better than Shakespeare's or compose music greater than Beethoven's or go to the planet Mars or become the first woman President—except, of course, that you wouldn't be nominated, let alone elected, because you're fat. . . ."

Dinah Randall, I thought, the first woman to be turned down by the party because she wouldn't go on a diet. . . .

"Brains," Walter Cronkite said over the evening news, "have been officially defined as *not enough*. It was unanimously agreed by Congress," he said, looking earnestly into the camera, "that thinness is the only thing that matters. An amendment to this effect has been ratified by all fifty states. . . . The U.N. is thinking of passing a resolution saying the same thing, only the Soviet Union and the Arab states have refused to sign. . . ."

The scene shifted to the U.N. The Soviet ambassador, followed by a lot of reporters, came out.

"Mr. Ambassador," a reporter said, holding a microphone in front of the ambassador's face, "how does the Soviet Union feel about the U.N. Resolution on Fat?"

The ambassador spoke in Russian to his interpreter. The interpreter said, "His Excellency, the ambassador, feels that Fat is a Capitalist Concept. . . ."

As I slugged through the grass, I wondered if I would be the first woman to defect to Moscow because of Fat. . . . Fat, Walter Cronkite said the following night on the news, had been declared by the President to be un-American. Even the civil liberty organizations had refused to defend Fat. . . .

I changed networks.

"The Randall family," David Brinkley announced, "has finally agreed to be interviewed." The camera now shifted to the Randall home. Our living room appeared on my mental TV screen.

Daddy and Jack were crying. Mother and Tony were looking thin and noble. Brenda was sitting in my chair, looking perfect and exceptionally thin. Donald wasn't there. "I knew, of course," Mother said, "that Dinah was going to defect, and it was a tragic and terrible decision to allow her to do so. But, as we all know, Fat has been declared un-American, so there was no hope for her in this country."

"Did she go alone?" David Brinkley asked, looking serious and thin.

"No," Mother said. "We allowed her to take her dog, Francis, who is also Fat. . . ."

At that point in my fantasy, and to my own surprise, I giggled. Then, when I imagined myself in Moscow, standing barefoot in drifts of snow in front of the American Embassy, staring at a sign saying in five languages NO FAT IN U.S., I started to cry again. I was patriotic, and did not want to have to defect to Russia because of Fat. . . .

A moment later I stumbled against the stump in

front of my tree and sat there, holding Francis inside my jacket. It had stopped raining, but it was damp and cool. I had come all this way so Francis and I could get up in the tree and go off into one of the Fat Kingdoms, or perhaps on the Spaceship *Francis*, as we had the other night. But I knew now that I was too tired to make the effort. Furthermore, sandals were not much use for leverage against a tree trunk.

"Oh, Francis," I said.

He whimpered and shivered again a little. I unzipped my jacket partway and put my hand on his coat. He was still wet. He should have been somewhere warm and dry where he could have some dinner and be quite sure that no one would send him to the pound. I zipped up my jacket again. For a while I sat there and held him. Then I got up, and cringed when some of my blisters stuck to my sandals. Holding Francis with one arm and my flashlight in my other hand, I went over to the rock and pulled it aside. I got out my notebook and pencil; I left the foot rule and put the rock back. Then I returned to the stump.

It was now completely dark, but I had my flashlight, so I sat on the stump and opened my notebook. Why, all of a sudden, I had to write, I didn't know. But I felt it was terribly important. So I moved Francis over to my left side, so I could hold him and the flashlight with my left hand and write with my right. But before I could even get started, Francis objected. He whimpered and wiggled and then uttered a short bark. The he scrambled out of my jacket and up on my shoulder before I knew what had happened.

"All right," I said. I lifted him off my shoulder and onto the ground.

The moment I put him down he squatted and peed. "Good boy!" I said.

But I didn't want him running off in the dark, so I put down my notebook, pencil and flashlight, and, feeling my way, snapped the leash onto his collar. Then I slipped the loop over my foot, and, wincing again, put my foot back down. But Francis must have been even tireder than I was. He didn't try to run away. He just sat there and uttered mournful whimpers. When I put my hand on him, I could feel that he was still a little wet and that he had started shivering again. Without lifting my foot, I stood up, took off my jacket, and understood immediately why my dress had been feeling so loose. Tony was right. Both side seams had ripped halfway down. Well, I thought, the dress had been nothing but a disaster anyway. I took off the dress and rubbed Francis with it. Then I put it back on, settled Francis on my jacket, which was more or less waterproof, and sat back down on the stump. Now I was the one who was shivering. But, despite that and the fact that my heart was broken and I wanted to die, I still had to write.

I started, "So the Green Fat King said to the Green Fat Queen, 'The trouble with Dinah is that she's not fat enough.'". . .

Usually this was all I needed to begin another adventure of the Green Fat Kingdom. But now I stared at the words and they meant nothing. In my head Their Green Fat Majesties just looked silly, like the illustrations on the playing cards my parents sometimes used.

I went on staring, trying to will the Green Fat Kingdom back. But nothing happened, and I had the strangest feeling that I would never again be able to lose myself in the Green Fat Kingdom, that it had gone somewhere else—or that perhaps I had.

So I wrote down my television fantasy, complete with the President's announcement about Fat, Congress, Walter, David and the Soviet ambassador. When that was finished I hesitated, then drew a line and wrote: "I am tired, tired, tired, tired of being fat."

Then, on the next line: "I am even more tired of people telling me that's all I am. Especially Mother."

After that, everything just seemed to fall out of my pencil:

> I wish I was dead (Not really, God. I just wish everybody thought I was and was very sorry for being mean to me. Especially Mother)
>
> I wish I had a boyfriend who thought I was terrific
>
> I wish Mother liked me better than Brenda
>
> I wish Brenda would go away and never come back
>
> I wish Tony would find out he had really been born to another family
>
> I wish I could write a great book that everybody would like and I'd be famous and be on television (only thin)
>
> I wish I was popular at school
>
> I wish I could run like Tony
>
> I wish I had a room in the attic to myself
>
> I wish I was thin

And then, without planning it at all, I started to write a story about Francis, and how he was dying, only nobody would tell me, and how, if only they had told me, I could have come and nursed him and he would have lived, but because he was a dog he couldn't ask for me. . . . And then somehow *I* was the one who was dying and someone had brought Francis so I could hold him and Mother was saying, "If only I had been nicer to her! It's all my fault. . . ."

My tears, falling on the page, were making it even wetter than the raindrops splashing from the leaves above. I gave a sob and turned the page and found that that had been the last one. There was no more notebook. I stared at the tan cover, and was about to write on that, when I noticed that the light from my flashlight seemed suddenly dim. If the battery died, there'd be no light at all.

All my fantasies went out of my head. I shone the dimming light on Francis and saw that he was not asleep. He was lying curled on my jacket, his eyes open, still shivering. If he got pneumonia and died it would be my fault. But if I took him home now, Mother would be so furious she would probably take him to the humane society tomorrow. And with my being out so late, I couldn't even be sure that Daddy would stick up for me. And I had been nasty to Jack, too.

As suddenly as my fantasies had gone, so did my grievance over how mean everyone at home had been. It was as though one door had closed and another had opened. All I could think of now was how terrible I had been. I had messed the gravy all over Tony, I had thrown the ball of paper towels at Mother—yes, I *had* thrown it at Mother, only I had missed—and I had run away and stayed for hours—how many, I had no idea. They would be so worried they'd be furious.

I leaned over, slid my jacket from under Francis, put it on and zipped it up. Then I picked him up, put him inside and tied the belt underneath. Then I slid the notebook in behind him.

"Come on, Francis," I said. "We're going to see Sebastian. You'll be safe there."

It was a long, damp climb up to the Van Hocht house, and my blisters hurt every step of the way. At one point I decided I might do better barefoot, and, with great difficulty, considering that Francis was like a camel's hump in the front of my jacket, succeeded in getting my sandals off. The trouble with that showed up a few steps later: I stepped on something sharp. "Ouch!" I said, standing on one foot. After another struggle, the sandals went back on again. The flashlight was still shining—but just barely. Luckily, I hit the road just as it went out. I saw my way through the Van Hochts' front gate and around to the back by the light of a streetlamp, and the lights showing from the house itself.

Most of those lights, I noticed, came from upstairs, though there was one on in what I thought was the library downstairs. But I decided to go around to the kitchen. I couldn't help having the feeling that if I turned up at the front door, the first thing anyone would do would be to telephone Mother, whereas if I sneaked into the back I might be able to talk to Sebastian without anybody's knowing. Also, in the kitchen there would be towels, and I could rub Francis dry. I was just sneaking past the side of the house when there was a deep, bone-crunching bark from inside. That was Diablo, of course. I stopped, frozen, while he went on barking, but after a few seconds it occurred to me that I could use the sound as a cover to run to the back, so I did. Diablo was still sounding as though he could hardly wait to grind our bones when I ran up the back stairs of the porch and pushed open the screen door. The test would be the kitchen door, which I was afraid would be locked. But it wasn't, and with Francis still in the front of my jacket I stepped inside.

For once I was lucky. Sebastian was there, in pajamas and a robe, kneeling beside a basket in the corner near the big range.

"Hi," I said.

He looked up. "What are you doing here?" he asked. "It's late."

"What time is it?"

"It's after ten. I'd be in bed, except that I'm looking after Napoleon."

"I have to dry off Francis," I said. "He got wet."

Sebastian got up as I put Francis on the floor. He was warm but still damp. "Do you have a towel?" I asked.

Sebastian opened a drawer and took out a folded towel. "Here. This is terry cloth," he said. Then he came over and leaned down and felt Francis. "How long has he been wet?" he asked.

"I don't know. Maybe a couple of hours."

"Why didn't you take him home or bring him up here right away? He might catch cold."

"Because I couldn't go home. I've run away. And I didn't bring him up here right away because I had to write something down, and anyway, I didn't realize that I would be coming up here. And I did try to dry him off. I used my dress. And I put him on my jacket while I was writing. I wouldn't do anything to hurt him, and you ought not to say I would."

"I didn't. What are you so upset about? What's the matter with you anyway?"

"I hate my family and I'm fat and they'll probably send Francis away and I forgot to feed him," I said, all in one breath, and burst into tears.

Sebastian took the towel out of my hands and bent down. "Come on, Francis," he said. "Let's rub you off."

I cried some more, feeling sad and happy as I watched Sebastian rub Francis's coat—happy because Sebastian was somebody who appreciated Francis, and sad because I knew I had come up here to leave him.

"I'll get him something to eat," Sebastian said. "Why is your family going to send Francis away?" He opened up a can of something, emptied it into a dish, and put the dish on the floor. Francis went over to it like a streak, and ate so fast it was practically like watching him inhale the food.

"Mother doesn't like him. She said that if I ate any sweets she'd take him away."

"Did you?"

"No. But I'm pretty sure that she'll be so mad at me for running away tonight that she'll make me get rid of Francis as a sort of punishment."

"That sounds terrible. Mom and my aunts wouldn't do that to Francis—or to any animal."

"That's because they're fat."

"What's that got to do with it?"

Now that he'd asked me, I didn't know. But I felt it was true anyway. After a minute I said, "I guess I mean they don't feel they have to be perfect or to made you perfect. And because they're fat, they're not always riding you about not being perfect, because they're not perfect themselves. So they can be nice to Francis, even though he's not beautiful and not very housebroken."

"Being fat is a lot better than having to have everybody perfect."

"Being fat isn't better than anything. It's worse than anything." I leaned down and started to rub Francis. And as I did that, what I had said hit me. I was fat, but Sebastian had cerebral palsy and often stammered badly, even though he wasn't stammering now. "I guess I shouldn't have said that," I said after a minute. "I'm sorry."

"Because I have a condition that's worse than being fat?"

Secretly I wondered if anything was worse than being fat. "At least people aren't telling you all the time that if you just do what they say you'll get over it. They don't think it's your fault."

"No. But it doesn't stop other k-kids from s-saying things, or imit-t-tating the way I walk."

When he talked about other kids, I noticed, his stammer came back. But I was puzzled by how ordinary his voice sounded otherwise. He didn't sound at all as though he were mad or hated them.

"Don't you care?" I asked.

"Sure. That's why I changed to St. Monica's. It got so I couldn't talk at all and they all thought I was retarded. I know it's a school for p-people who are different, but I'm different and I might just as well get used to it. And if I want to do things I'm interested in, like being a vet, I can't be stewing all the time about how other people think." He got up, went to a cupboard and got out a cardboard carton. Then he put some fresh towels in it. "Francis can sleep here, if you want. I'll look after him. But I don't think you ought to just give in like that."

"Well, what can I do if Mother decides she's just going to take him away?"

"You can at least put up a fight. You can talk to her. If she's already called the humane society to come and get him, then you can bring him up here. But I bet Francis would stick up for you better than you're sticking up for him."

"And what if she does it from the office while I'm at school? She could tell them to pick him up and order Mrs. Lewis to hand him over."

"Boy, she must be a monster!"

"She is *not!*"

"Well, you're the one who's saying what she'd do. I've heard of parents like that. But I've never actually met one. Mom and my aunts may be too fat, but at least they're human. Your mother doesn't even sound human. What about your father?"

"He's great!"

"Wouldn't he stand up for Francis?"

"Yes, but—"

"But what? Is your mother the only one who has any say?"

I didn't say anything, because I was having a funny, topsy-turvy feeling. All of a sudden I was thinking about things I had forgotten, like the time I'd had measles, and my eyes had hurt, and I hadn't been allowed to read or watch television, so Mother had taken her vacation and stayed home so she could read to me for days and days. And because I hadn't been able to bear much light, she had read aloud in a dark room with only one small light. Then there was the time when a teacher accused me of copying something from the girl next to me. I came home and told Mother. She asked me if I had done it, and when I told her I hadn't, she came to school the next morning and told the teacher off and made her admit that she'd just been guessing. Another time when Mother was between jobs, she and I would sit at the kitchen table in the afternoon when I got home from school and share a peanut butter and jelly sandwich and talk.

"She's not a monster," I said. "Things seem mixed up. She hates my being fat. I guess she's right. It's better to be thin. But all she *ever* talks about is my weight."

"I don't care if you're fat. I like you a lot better than any of those kids at the school you're going to."

"You do?"

"Sure. The others are stupid. All they talk about is themselves and who's on what team. And they play games on people. At least you care about animals. Sister Elizabeth says you have a lot of imagination. Maybe that's what happens. You imagine things and then you think that's the way they really are."

A nice feeling spread over me. "I like you, too, Sebastian."

"Yeah?"

"Yes."

There wasn't much light in the kitchen, but it looked to me as though he was blushing. He took off his glasses and polished them on the towel he'd been using to wipe Francis. All of a sudden it struck me that he was quite good-looking.

The door opened and Miss Amelia Van Hocht came in. "Sebastian—" she started. Then she saw Francis and me. Francis had gone to sleep on the floor about six inches from his dish.

"Dinah, what are you doing here?"

I opened my mouth but nothing came out, so I closed it again.

"Does your family know where you are?"

I shook my head. "No."

"Do you know what time it is?"

I cleared my throat. "Around ten."

"It is ten-thirty. How did you get here?"

I took a breath. "I got mad and ran away and have been walking with Francis around the field."

"And how long ago did you run away?"

"I guess—it was during dinner."

"And you've been walking around in the field in the dark ever since?"

"Yes."

She was looking at me very sharply. "Alone?"

"Yes," I said.

"All right." Her eye wandered to my foot. "What did you do to your foot?"

I glanced down. There was red on one of my sandals and more smeared on my foot. "I took off my sandals for a bit and stepped on something sharp. I guess that's blood."

"You'd better let me look at it. Sit down on the chair there. But before I do anything else, I'm going to call your parents. They must be terribly worried." As she moved towards the phone on the wall, the robe she was wearing sort of billowed out behind her. It was funny, I thought. She was enormous, and yet she looked nice.

"I'm afraid Mother's going to be furious," I blurted out.

"I wouldn't be surprised. I'd be furious too. Worry often has that effect."

"Yes—but . . ."

She had her hand on the receiver. "But what?"

"You wouldn't take Francis away as punishment."

"I might."

"No you wouldn't, Aunt Amelia," Sebastian burst out. "You'd never do a thing like that."

"I can't judge what I'd do if I were somebody else altogether, and you can't either." She looked at me. "Is that what you ran away about? Francis?"

"No. It was because . . . because I'm too fat and Mother's always at me about it. But I lost five pounds and tried to tell her she wouldn't even listen. All she did was be nice to my cousin, Brenda."

"Maybe she felt your cousin needed her attention more than you did."

"Brenda's a creep. But Mother likes her much better than she does me."

"I would be willing to bet you that she doesn't. But you're going to have to find that out from her. And running away is never a solution to anything. The problem doesn't go away. You have to stay and fight it out. What's your number?"

Grumpily, I told her. She lifted the receiver and dialed. After a minute I heard her say, "Mr. Randall? This is Amelia Van Hocht. Dinah is here." There was a pause. "Yes, apart from a cut on her foot, she seems all right. Very well, then we'll see you in a few minutes." She hung up the receiver. "Your father is coming to get you."

"Did he sound mad?"

"He sounded relieved, which often takes the form of being mad." She went over to a drawer and took out a box. "Now let's look at that foot."

It was after she'd disinfected the cut and put a

bandage on it and bandages on my blisters that she said, "You should probably have a tetanus shot. Tell your mother, and she can take you to your doctor."

"Miss Van Hocht," I burst out, "why are people so horrible to other people about being fat?"

"Because, unfortunately, it's an unpleasant aspect of human nature to pick on any oddity, anything that makes a person different." She glanced at me. "I don't suppose it's much comfort to you, but two hundred years ago Sebastian here might well have been stoned. He would certainly have been publicly made fun of. Did you know that in the eighteenth century in London people used to go on Sundays and holidays to laugh at the poor, deranged inmates of Bethlehem Hospital—known as Bedlam? Laughing at others, or mocking them, or making them feel uncomfortable is what makes some people feel superior. At least in one respect society has improved—laughing at the mentally ill or crippled is not considered socially acceptable today. But fat people are still thought of as fair game."

"It's *not* fair!"

"Well," Miss Van Hocht said, putting the box away, "as one of our Presidents said, there's really no such thing as fair or unfair. It's the way it is. And, Dinah, you're going to have to accept it and make your choice. I've been thin and I've been fat, and there's no question, thin is better. But sometimes staying thin has been more than I can manage, like now. And when that happens, you have to refuse to allow people to get to you and run your life."

"How?"

The doorbell rang.

"Sebastian, would you get that?" Miss Van Hocht said.

As he left the kitchen, she said to me, "I guess the best answer I can give you is to remember to respect yourself, no matter what size or shape you are. No matter who says what. And that's easy to say, but it takes a lot of doing."

A minute later Sebastian came back in, followed by my father.

SEVEN

For what seemed like several minutes Daddy and I stared at each other. Miss Van Hocht finally said, "Sebastian, it's time you were in bed."

"I'll just check on Napoleon," he said, and limped to the corner of the room.

"Dinah," my father said, "where have you been?"

"In . . . in the fields. I took a walk."

"You were in the fields, by yourself, in the dark, for nearly three hours?"

"It wasn't dark all the time." I paused. "Are you mad at me?"

He had been standing, looking stiff and tight, but he seemed suddenly to loosen up, and he came over and put his hands on my shoulders. "If you ever do that again—scare me, us, like that—I . . . I don't know what I'll do." Then he hugged me, almost lifting me off the floor and squeezing me tight. "There were at least half a dozen occasions tonight when, if I could have laid hands on you, I would have beaten you black and blue in the worst tyrannical-father tradition. We're all going to have to get a few things straightened out, but right now, let's get back. Your poor mother is sitting at home frantic with worry and self-reproach. Now come on. Let's go." He turned then to Miss Van Hocht. "And thank you for calling me. My wife and I really appreciate it. Dinah, you coming?"

"Just a minute," I said. I went over to the corner. "Sebastian—" I started. Then I stopped. In the basket was a tortoiseshell cat, black, white, and orange, with six brand-new kittens vigorously feeding at her nipples.

"*Napoleon?*" I said.

"That's what her name was on her collar when we found her. See?" Sebastian reached up and took a collar off the cabinet. Sure enough, on one side of a small metal disc was the name Napoleon. "Whoever named her didn't know much about cats."

"You mean couldn't tell what sex it was."

"No. I mean three-colored cats are almost always female."

"Always?"

"*Almost* always."

"Oh."

"Would you like a kitten later?"

"No, thanks. I have Francis." I paused. "And thanks for what you said . . . you know what I mean."

Once again I thought I could see Sebastian's cheeks grow pink. "It's okay."

"Come on, Francis," I said firmly. I got his leash out of my pocket and snapped it on his collar. Then I stood up. "I'm bringing Francis home with me," I said to Daddy.

"Of course. Why not?"

"Because I thought Mom . . . Mom might make me get rid of him because I ran away." I glanced at Sebastian, who was watching me. "But I don't think that's right, and I'm going to stick up for him."

"Fine. I don't know what, if anything, your mother intends to impose by way of punishment. You'll have to talk to her about it. But I agree that you should present his case." He frowned. "Are you saying this because you were intending to leave Francis here?"

"Yes. I thought Mother would send him away. And I knew that Sebastian would take good care of him. But then Sebastian said I shouldn't just run away. I should put up a fight."

"Sebastian is one thousand percent right." He hesitated. "I say that fully aware of the fact that speaking up for yourself hasn't been made very easy for you. I'm sorry about that, Dinah, and I know your mother is, too. But we'll talk about that later." He turned towards Sebastian. "Come and see us." He glanced at Miss Van Hocht. "And thanks again."

"You didn't drive?" I asked when we got outside.

"No. Once your mother was convinced you were all right, she agreed to let me walk up here. I wanted to have a chance to talk to you."

"Okay. But I have blisters and I can't walk that fast."

"That's all right. We can go slow."

The rain had stopped and some of the clouds had gone. There were big patches of stars that were reflected, along with the streetlights, in the puddles on the road. Francis was too sleepy and tired to pull on the leash. He just trotted along quietly beside me.

Daddy had said he wanted to talk to me. But for a while he didn't say anything. He just took my hand and held it in his as we walked.

Finally I burst out, "Do you think Mother will be very angry?"

"I'm not going to comment on that, Dinah. I've been telling you your mother loves you, and you haven't believed a word I've said. And I've told your mother that I think she's handling this weight problem of yours the wrong way, and she doesn't believe me about that. I'm sick of interpreting one of you to the other. You're going to have to talk to each other and work it out for yourselves."

We walked in silence some more. What Daddy had said seemed sort of like what Sebastian had said. "You mean, I shouldn't run away."

"That's right. If you have a problem and feel that you're not being treated fairly, then you should talk it out." He squeezed my hand. "As I said before, I realize that hasn't always been made easy for you."

"I tried. People don't listen."

"I'm listening now. The floor is yours."

The funny part was, when he said that, everything seemed to dry up.

"Come on, Dinah. Speak. I know you feel you have a genuine grievance, and I want to hear what it is, from you. Furthermore, I'm in your corner."

"I'm tired of being fat!" I burst out. "But I guess I'm even tireder of people talking about it. I said that to Miss Van Hocht, and she said that people always laughed at people who were different, or made comments about them, and that is was human nature or something. She said that two hundred years ago they used to openly make fun of people who were crippled or insane, or people like Sebastian, but they don't do that anymore. They just do it now to people who're fat. And when I said it was unfair, she said that was the way things were. And the only thing I can do about it is to respect myself whether I'm fat or thin."

"She's right."

I didn't say anything.

Daddy squeezed my hand again. "I know that's easy to say. Go on."

"What I don't understand is why everybody thinks it's okay to tell me I ought to lose weight or . . . or make other remarks, or tease me—Mother, the kids at school and Tony tease me—when it's not okay to talk about something else. And I don't mean what Miss Van Hocht was talking about, like being lame or insane. There's a boy at school who has a huge nose, like that character in a French play."

"Cyrano?"

"Yes. That's the one. Well, once, in class, I don't know why it came up, but one of the kids made a comment about it, and everybody giggled. And the teacher gave us this long lecture on how awful and uncivilized it was to make what she called 'personal remarks.' She said you shouldn't ever do it to anybody. But a week later, when I was throwing a Frisbee in the school yard and split my shirt, she was passing and said, 'Watch those calories!' and everybody laughed."

"Did you remind her of what she'd said about personal remarks?"

"No. Everybody was listening and they just would have laughed harder."

"Well, to be fair," Daddy said, "it's the kind of off-the-cuff comment that she might have made to anybody who'd just split a seam. The trouble is, if you'd been skinny, you wouldn't have found it such a loaded remark. But—and I know you hate to hear this—she might feel that the boy can't do anything about his nose, whereas you can do something about your weight."

"People have their noses fixed."

"True. But not generally when they're of school age. Or at least so I understand. However, you do have a point about a double standard, and about people making insensitive comments. I know; I've made some myself."

He hesitated and then went on. "In between bouts of wanting to throttle you this evening, I thought a lot about what you said at dinner and your problem with your weight, which is what brought all this on. And I came to the conclusion that your problem is really two problems—related, obviously, but different.

"The first one is the easier one, the mechanical one: so many calories of food in, so many calories of energy out. What's left over becomes your bugbear and torment—fat. But it is, as I said, basically a mechanical problem. The second problem is much worse: it is your anger over people's attitudes and the fact that they feel so free to comment on your weight, tease you about it, and judge you because of it. As Miss Van Hocht told you, some people do feel free to make life difficult for anybody who deviates from the norm. It's certainly one of the less attractive aspects of human nature. And the ironic part is that, say, seventy-five years ago, you wouldn't have had anywhere near the same amount of trouble. Fashion is powerful, and plump ladies were fashionable then. If you're curious, you could go to the library and look up the fashion

drawings in magazines around the turn of the century.
. . . But Dinah, my darling child—" he squeezed my
hand again —"it is your luck, or ill luck, I'm not sure
which, to have come along at a time when fashion
says you have to be thin."

"Why luck?" I said angrily. "I think it's a lousy
deal."

"Look, Dinah, most medical authorities today agree
that it's healthier to be thin than to be overweight. So
it could be argued that those who are badgered into
conforming to that standard are better off, physically
at least, than if they had lived at an earlier time when
they could be fat in peace. But there have been mo-
ments lately when I've wondered if the psychological
damage doesn't outbalance the physical good. I just
don't know. A woman I know—she used to work in our
office—once went on a diet and lost fifty pounds. She
told me afterwards that when the loss started to show,
everybody complimented her, and at first she loved it.
Then she started to resent it. And she ended up thin,
but as angry as you are now. She said that as people
went on and on, telling her how marvelous she looked
and how great she was, she felt that they were telling
her that because she now conformed to their standard,
she was okay. And she felt like yelling back at them
that she was exactly the same person inside and that
if she was acceptable now, she'd been acceptable before, and to get off judging her."

" 'I'll be judge, I'll be jury,' " I muttered.

"*Alice in Wonderland?*"

"Yes."

"I remember your mother reading that aloud. Dinah, honey, there's one thing I do know. You're not
going to change other people. If you try, you'll just

break your head or your heart or both. The only place where you have the power to make a change is within you. Are you listening to me?"

"Yes," I said glumly.

"You can diet and lose weight, if that is what you decide to do—and I, personally, believe that making your own decision is the only way you'll ever do it. Or you can choose to stay fat and accept yourself as you are. And when I say accept, I mean like yourself and, as Miss Van Hocht said, respect yourself, fat or thin. If you can manage to do that, to stand by your own choice, to respect its dignity, then what people say can't get to you. Now, when somebody says something ugly about your weight, there's a Judas within you, a small betraying voice that says, 'They're right.' And that inner voice piles on the self-hatred. When somebody says, 'You're fat,' that inner Judas doesn't let it go at that. It says, 'And that means loathsome and unlovable and unloved.' Dinah, all the people in the world couldn't do to you what you do to yourself."

We were walking more slowly now, coming down towards the bend that led to our road. And I was crying and looking for a tissue. "I thought it was what people did to you when you were little that counted."

"Only up to a point. Here, take this," Daddy handed me his handkerchief. "And you're long past that point. You're at the beginning of adolescence. From now on, it's your show. The most your mother and I can do is to give you love and support."

"Mother doesn't support me."

"In her way, she thought that was what she was doing. She was going hell for leather after the medical fact—thin is better than fat. And she did that not because she's cruel, and certainly not because she doesn't love you. But by nature and temperament and training, she focuses on the objective fact, rather than seeking the subjective feeling behind the fact. Remember, she's a mathematician and an economist, not a psychologist."

"You're not a psychologist, but you understand." I stopped. We were about to leave the main road and go into the road leading to our house.

"No, but I guess that's not the point, either. It's a matter of temperament and slant of mind. One kind is not better than another. Just different. . . . One final thing." He put his arms around me and held me close. "No parent is supposed to say this, and if you quote me, I'll deny it. But Dinah, you're my favorite. I love you best. And I love you no matter what, whether you're fat or thin or beautiful or plain or successful or not successful. It doesn't matter. I love you now, and I will love you always. And don't ever forget it."

I really did cry then. I just bawled against Daddy's sweater. I cried and cried. It was only when my nose started to run that I finally pulled away to blow it.

"Now let's go home," Daddy said.

Somehow, and no matter what Daddy had said about Mother's being full of self-reproach, I was quite sure she'd be madder than she'd ever been before. So I wasn't prepared to catch one glimpse of her tear-stained face, and then be bear-hugged so tightly that I almost couldn't breathe.

"I'm sorry, Mom. Truly I am," I said, astounded to realize it was quite true.

"I strongly suggest," Daddy said, hovering in the hall, "that we all go to bed. Now. And leave further postmortems till tomorrow."

"Oh, lambie," Mother said, ignoring him. "I didn't mean to be such a beast. I just have this terrible tendency to get an idea in my head and bird-dog it to death."

"Tomorrow," Daddy said.

"Mom," I said, "you aren't going to send Francis away, are you? I mean, I know I promised about not eating sweets, but I just don't want to have to think that if I eat a candy bar he's going to be exterminated or given away. I mean, I love him."

"No, darling, of course not. I shouldn't have ever made that a condition. It was just part of some terrific master plan that I got into my head. I shouldn't have held that over you. It was terribly stupid and wrong."

"Don't cry, Mom. Here, take this." And I handed her the handkerchief Daddy had lent me.

"I do love you," Mother said, turning the handkerchief around to find a dry place. "Please don't ever think again that I don't." She blew her nose.

"Bed," Daddy said. "I'm taking Dinah up right now."

"Yes, all right. Your father's right. We'll talk tomorrow. Good night, my darling. Don't run away again. I couldn't stand it."

"Come along, Dinah," Daddy said. He was halfway up the stairs.

"I know the way," I said.

"No, you don't."

I couldn't figure out what he meant until I started to go in the direction of the room that Brenda and I shared.

"No," Daddy said. "Up here." He was standing at the foot of the attic stairs. He started up and Francis and I followed. "By the way," he said, glancing back, "this was your mother's idea. The whole thing."

When we got to the top and opened the door, I saw that the bed in the attic had been made up, and I could see some of my clothes hanging in an old wardrobe. "I'm calling the roofer tomorrow," Daddy said, "and Tony and I can move your furniture—that is, if you want to stay up here. If you want your old room, then we can put Brenda up here. It will be your choice. Your mother insisted on that. Your mother said she'd make up the bed here while I was going to get you, because she thought it would be easier for you to be up here by yourself tonight. Good night, Dinah. I think you and Francis will sleep soundly. By the way, we put some paper down in the corner for him." He kissed me good night and closed the attic door behind him.

I looked around. Francis had made it as far as the bed and was sound asleep at the foot of it. I was suddenly so tired that I was tempted not to undress at all. But at least I would take off my jacket. I untied my belt and unzipped my jacket and the notebook fell to the floor. I was too tired to pick it up. My dress practically fell to the floor, too. I put on my nightgown, slid into the bed and was asleep before I pulled the covers up. I was wiped out.

"Dinah."

I opened my eyes. Mother was sitting on my bed holding a glass of orange juice. "Good morning," she said, and held out the glass.

I sat up and took the orange juice and drank all of it. It tasted wonderful. "Thanks," I said. And then: "What time is it?"

"Ten-thirty."

"Ten-*thirty!* But what about school?"

"I called and said you wouldn't be in till later. I thought we might have a talk."

As I stared at her, everything about the previous night came back. "Okay," I said. I looked at her carefully to see if she was, after all, angry, and then looked down into my lap. As far as I could see she wasn't, but I was feeling cautious. And then I thought of something else. "What about your job? You haven't gone to work!"

"I called them and gave them the same message."

"Oh." I took a breath. "Okay."

"Dinah, you remind me of somebody standing in front of a firing squad with her eyes closed saying 'Okay, shoot!' " Mother sighed. "But I guess I have myself to thank for that." She took the glass from my hand and put it on the floor beside the bed. Then she sat up and took both of my hands in hers. "Let's begin at the beginning. I love you very much. And I'm sorrier than I can tell you that I made you feel that the only thing about you that I thought about or noticed was your weight. And that I made you think I cared for Brenda more than I do you. It's simply not true, either one."

"Then why did you act that way?"

"I don't really know, Dinah. It's the crazy upside-down way parents sometimes behave. They lay themselves out to be nice to other people's children, whom they don't really like, and are harsh with their own, whom they love. It's something to do with that terrible scourge, perfectionism. 'My child has to be perfect. And I'll badger her until she gets that way.' It's awful." Mother paused. "My own father did that to me. So I should know better."

"About being fat?"

"No. Although I was when I was a teenager."

"You *were?* Why didn't you say so? You've always been thin since I can remember."

"I guess I never talked about it because I hated it so much that in some way or other I blocked it out. I finally got the weight off when I was about sixteen, and I was determined that nobody in future would ever know I'd been fat. I even went through Mother's family album and destroyed all the old snapshots of me from the time I was about twelve till I got thin at sixteen." She paused. "Last night, after you'd been gone a while, and I didn't know where you were, I remembered it."

"How did you get thin?"

"I decided I wanted to be thin, and so I went on a diet. And I guess that's really the secret—that *I* decided it. Nobody decided it for me. My parents didn't care that much. They just said, 'Oh, it'll come off one of these days,' when anybody mentioned it. On that subject, anyway, I didn't feel pushed into a corner."

I pulled up my knees. "I thought you just said your father was a perfectionist."

"Not about that. I was bright and he wanted me to get perfect grades. That kind of thing." She looked at me. "Your father says that I'm what psychologists call task-oriented, rather than person-oriented. I wanted you to be thin, I guess, partly because of my own history in that area, and also because it's healthier to be thin, and I knew you'd feel happier that way. But in worrying about the pounds that had to come off, I forgot to think about how you might feel. When you resisted me, well, then you were just being stubborn. I know it sounds crazy, but I think that at some point I acted as though I thought you were a computer that would automatically come up with the right answer if I fed it the right information. And James—your father—worried about your feelings. It's so funny, Dinah, because conventional wisdom and tradition state that it's the other way around—it's men who are supposed to see the job first and the person second, and women who fuss over how people feel.

"I still want you to be thinner, for all the reasons that I've mentioned, but I've come to see that harassing you and embarrassing you is not the way to do it—not that I meant to embarrass you, Dinah, truly. I'm not tactful—I never have been. And to be truthful, I don't think I'm going to change all that much. I'll try, because I love you and because I want us to be friends. If parents aren't friends with their children by the time the children are in their teens, then the outlook for the future relationship is pretty dismal, because there's not much parenting left to go."

She paused. When I didn't say anything because couldn't think of anything to say, she went on. "About Brenda, I think the accusation that I loved her more than I did you was the worst of all. I lay awake most of the night and thought about it and tried to see how it looked from your point of view. And I realized then that you couldn't know why I was acting the way I was. You see, I've always felt sorry for her. I don't think it's maternal bias when I say that I've never thought she had one-tenth of your brains or vitality or attractiveness. But I've been so busy harping on your weight, I forgot to tell you that I've always thought you were pretty outstanding. Brenda is a mouse. The trouble is, she's a jealous mouse—eaten up with envy of you."

"Of *me!*"

"Yes. Of you. Can you imagine your father deciding to stay away for two years and not see you? He'd tell all the oil and mineral and mining companies in the world to go fly a kite first. You must know that."

The moment she said it, I did. Even when I was staying with Granny when he and Mother were away, he'd find excuses to fly home and see me. I thought then of what he'd said the night before on the walk home. It was something warm and delicious to hold, like a heating pad on a cold night.

"Then," Mother went on, "there's the fact that I've always carried around a guilt complex about Brenda's mother, my younger sister. I went ahead and did a lot of things and was a big shot at school and college and became pretty successful. She had a tougher time. I could have helped her, but I didn't. I was too busy winning prizes and scholarships and grants and trips. And, to be truthful—" Mother looked down at her hands—"I found her pretty boring. I've never put that into so many words before, even in my mind, but on some level I knew it, and felt guilty about it. I guess I've been trying to make up to Brenda for that."

Suddenly Brenda didn't seem such a creep. I rested my chin on my knees. "I'll try to get on better with her," I said. "Maybe she's not as awful as I thought."

Mother sighed. "She probably is. But she might blossom a bit if you'd give her a little approval. I must say, yesterday was not her day. To cap that letter from her father and that awful dinner, Jack made her an apple-pie bed."

I giggled. "Why?"

"I think to avenge your honor."

"I got cross at him, too."

"He understood. He's very like your father, you know. And he adores you. You're just about his favorite person."

"Even if I'm fat." The words were out before I knew it.

"Oh, darling, being fat doesn't have anything to do with people loving you."

I swung my legs over the side of the bed. "Yes, it does. When people tease you and make fun of you, they're not loving you. At least not what I think about as loving. And then when they say 'Oh, we don't care whether you're fat or thin,' it's a lie. Anyway, with most people it is. If you're fat they treat you different." I thought a minute. "A little like Sebastian, Miss Van Hocht's nephew. He goes to St. Monica's too, because he has cerebral palsy, although it doesn't show that much now. He says that because he stammers and walks in a funny way, most people think he can't do anything. And it's not true. He's very bright and he does a lot. He's in charge of all the animals at St. Monica's. That's why—" Suddenly I looked around. "Where's Francis?"

"I took him out for a little walk earlier, and gave him some breakfast. To keep him quiet while I talked to you, I bribed him with a beef bone." She got up and opened the attic door. A small, plump, lion-colored dog with a mashed-in nose flew in and onto the bed.

"Francis!" I said joyfully, and gave him a hug.

"I'll get you some breakfast," Mother said from the door.

"Fine. Mom—"

Mother had been about to go out, but she turned.

For a second it had flashed throught my mind that I would tell Mother that I was thinking of taking up running. And then I knew that Sister Elizabeth was right: it should be my secret. At least for a while. I'd wait until I'd tried it and tested myself. If I told Mother now, it could so easily become something she'd start asking me about. "Dinah, have you run today? How far?" And then I would begin to hate it. Not because it was Mother, but because it would be something I would have to do, because somebody would be asking me about it.

"Yes?" Mother said. She was still at the door.

"I'm sorry, well, half sorry I said all those things and ran away. But maybe if I hadn't, we wouldn't have talked."

"I'm sorry that I've said and done the things I've done, too, Dinah. I'm not sure that at this point I can radically change my spots. The leopard remains the leopard. So you're just going to have to try to remember that, and when I start bird-dogging something the way I do, tell me that I'm doing it. And I'll try to stop. And I'll also try to help you instead of push you. Because your father is right—from here on out, and no matter what I happen to think, what you'll be happiest doing or being is really your decision. And you have to know that. And so do I. Together, we'll manage. That's the main thing—not to shove blindly ahead, which is my tendency, or to run away, which is yours, but to work it out."

It was odd. I'd always thought of Mother as powerful. But now, standing at the door there, she looked rather small and uncertain. I put Francis to one side and went over and put my arms around her. We hugged each other in silence for a minute. Then

Mother cleared her throat and said, "I forgot to tell you something. When I came in early this morning to take Francis out, I found a notebook in the middle of the floor. I hope you don't mind, but I read it."

"Oh," I said, not sure what I thought about that.

"You write extremely well. I hadn't realized how good you were. Parts of it were very funny. I particularly liked your television fantasy, although I certainly don't want you to defect to Russia for any reason whatsoever. Or to anywhere else. You know, you could write a book—or a play, maybe—about the Green Fat Kingdom."

"Do you really think so?"

"I don't see why not. And I hope you get at least some of that rather touching list of wishes."

I thought about them. "Well," I said, "I may have gotten one, sort of."

"Oh? That's good. Which one?"

"Sebastian didn't actually say he thought I was terrific. But he said he liked me better than any of the other kids in my school."

"He's a man of taste. Why don't we invite him to lunch? Maybe on Saturday?"

"That'd be nice."

"By the way, do you want to stay up here, or have your old room downstairs?"

"I'd rather stay up here. I like it. Mom, do you *really* think I could write a book about the Green Fat Kingdom?"

"I don't see why not. Give it a try."

I suddenly remembered another on my list of wishes: that I'd write a book and become famous and be interviewed on television (only thin). Perhaps I would really start seriously thinking about a diet.

"How lucky it is that Francis isn't a greyhound," Mother said, glancing down at Francis, who had jumped off the bed and was busy trying to ambush the rag rug.

"Why?" I asked suspiciously.

"Because with his general figure and shape, you could cast him as the Green Fat Prince. The role suits him to perfection. Come along down and have some breakfast."